DOUBT

Brenda Holland

First published in Great Britain by Pen Press

All paper used in the printing of this book has been made from wood grown in managed, sustainable forests.

ISBN: 978-1-78003-806-3

Printed and bound in the UK

Pen Press is an imprint of
Author Essentials
4 The Courtyard
South Street
Falmer
East Sussex
BN1 9PQ

A catalogue record of this book is available from the British Library

Cover design by Jacqueline Abromeit

For

Beverley, Sally and David and
my husband Alastair,
my love and gratitude for
their loving care and unfailing support.

The secret for health both in mind and body is not to mourn for the past, worry about the future or anticipate troubles that may never come but to live for the moment as wisely and as well as you can.

Chapter 1

Yesterday

The quiet calm of the office was broken. Damn! Just what she didn't need! Karis Fielden picked up the phone on its third ring, tucking her hair behind her ear and glancing at the clock as she did so.

"Good afternoon. Oliver Melrose's office," she said, her voice giving away nothing of the irritation she felt but managing to convey to the caller that he had her full attention.

"Hello Karis. Hugo Smith. How are you?" and then, not waiting for her answer, "Is Oliver available for a quick word?"

"Hello, Sir Hugo. No, I'm sorry he isn't. At the moment, he's right in the middle of a video conference with his Finance Director and I think it is unlikely that he will be finished with that for some time yet. Can I take a message for him or get him to give you a call in the morning?"

Hugo Smith was one of Oliver's closest business associates and he was also a personal friend of both Oliver and his wife Kate. Karis liked him. Unlike some of Oliver's business friends and acquaintances, he was always polite, pleasant and easy to talk to and if, as rumour had it, he could be an awkward customer to deal with, then that was a side of him that she had never seen, heard or had to deal with.

The all important video conference was with the CEO of a hair products company and his directors. Oliver was in the process of trying to buy the company, the acquisition process having reached the final offer stage and was therefore delicately poised between success and failure, and he had given Karis strict instructions that under no circumstances was he to be disturbed while the call was in progress.

"I see." There was a short silence while Hugo's thought process went into operation (Karis could almost hear the wheels in motion) and then he said, "Well it was nothing very important Karis, so it will keep until tomorrow. I was just wondering whether Oliver plans to go to the club's AGM next week. I thought perhaps we could travel together if he is. I'll ring again in the morning and have a word with him then. I hope you are keeping well," and again, without waiting for her answer, he rang off.

Karis flipped through the diary to check that the AGM date had been pencilled in. It had and she made a note to mention to Oliver that Sir Hugo had phoned. They often travelled to London together for special occasions at their club as it gave them a chance to chew over the business world and also keep up with personal gossip en route, without the hindrance of the constant interruptions they would get if in their respective offices.

Karis looked at the clock again; time was racing by as it does when you have a deadline to meet. She and Jonathan, her husband, were scheduled to go to their daughter's school that evening to see the annual play which, this year, was being directed by Joanne, and Karis, having promised that she wouldn't be late, was anxious to leave the office at a reasonable hour - 6.30 at the latest and it was now 5.50.

For the past two years, Joanne had played a leading role in the play and enjoyed doing so but this year she had been asked if she would like to try her hand at directing and, much to her surprise, she had found that she was getting more from the experience than she did from acting. Naturally, Karis and Jonathan wanted to give her their support so Karis needed to get home as soon as possible to make sure that she had time to collect Jonathan before going on to see the play and that they were not late for the start. It was also important that she should make an effort to spend some quality time with him and to let him know that he was still her number one priority. He had been surprisingly tolerant of her recent extra long days in the office, often getting dinner for them both when she had been working late. Karis often found herself torn between her priorities, not wanting to fail to give both family and her job her best.

It had been a frantically busy time in the office over the past couple of months while the ifs and buts of the proposed acquisition had been discussed and identified, then analysed and finishing touches and last minute adjustments had been made to the takeover plan. The company's plans, naturally, had to be kept secret so only a few members of the company were aware of their intention to buy the hair products company which, if successful, would dovetail very nicely in with their present range of cosmetics and toiletries, and would create expansion and growth at a time when business was sluggish and difficult.

The hair products company had now been formally approached with their offer to buy it and Oliver and his directors were waiting with barely concealed impatience and anxiety to hear whether their initial offer had been favourably received or was likely to be turned down. They had reached the critical stage of negotiations, which was why the video conference was currently going on in Oliver's office.

Fingers were being kept very firmly crossed and there was a barely concealed air of excitement and optimism within the small group of people who knew what was going on. It would be a huge relief to Oliver to be able to tell the workforce of the acquisition, if it was successful of course, that their company was likely to double in size and that jobs were also likely to be secured. The few people who were actively involved in the acquisition had all been working long hours, getting extra and necessary work done, often after normal office hours so that the offer would be one that would be very difficult to turn down and, not surprisingly, little niggles and signs of strain and extreme tiredness were beginning to show up in short tempers and a thinly-veiled strained atmosphere between them.

At that moment, there was a knock on the office door and the dark curly hair and eager-faced head of the Strategic Planning Department appeared round her door. "Still here then?" it said, grinning at her.

"Perceptive as always, Alan. Come in," Karis replied, hoping that he wasn't going to be a nuisance and need her to do something she didn't have time for, but smiling as she spoke, softening her sarcasm. "What can I do for you?"

They were outwardly friendly towards each other but Karis never saw him without remembering the occasion when the Strategic Planning group had been at an off-site meeting for a couple of days which necessitated an overnight stay and he had approached her during a collective post-meeting drink the first evening and whispered his room number in her ear! She had been taken by surprise, openly laughed in his face and told him to go and play with his toys.

Since then and because of that incident, Karis didn't particularly like him. However, she couldn't fault his manners towards her and he was always polite when speaking to her. It was just that he was too damn full of himself and his know-it-all manner irritated her too, always with a smile on his face and ready with a smart remark. Why couldn't he be normal and have the odd bad day like everyone else? She grudgingly conceded, though, that he was good at his job and as far as Oliver was concerned, that was what mattered; what he got up to in his own time was up to him and, of course, Oliver would never know about Alan's approach to her at the off-site meeting.

"I need to see Oliver tomorrow morning, urgently. A problem has come up and I must clear with him what action I take before I do anything." Alan's face was serious, his tone urgent.

Karis looked at the diary on her desk again, one page per day and with little space in it the following day. "He can give you ten minutes at 11.30. Is that any good?"

He pondered the question for a moment as if it was vitally important which, to him, it probably was and then said, "Yes. Thanks. See you then," and he was gone.

Karis's office was roughly 12ft by 10ft with a door opening into it from a corridor which lead to the other five directors' offices on one side with a large open plan office on the other. Another door on the opposite wall, took you into Oliver's office; there was no other way in which meant that all traffic to and from Oliver had to go past Karis.

Her office was furnished with matching light oak filing cupboards and an L-shaped desk and was carpeted in fawn brown with a green fleck, which toned in with the muted olive green colour of the walls; a pair of water colours of some leafy glades and heath land of the New

Forest were hung on the wall opposite Karis's desk. They had been bought by Oliver as a birthday present for her and, as she had chosen them herself, she was particularly fond of them. An easy chair upholstered in dark cream leather was just in front of the window which was to the side of the office overlooking the car park and part of the gardens, which were mostly laid to lawn with flowering shrubs and trees in island beds. The gardens were to the front of the office block and the factory where all the company products were manufactured was immediately behind the office block.

Karis sat at her desk looking out of the window, impatient for something to happen soon so she could get away otherwise she was going to be late. And then, fortunately, a few minutes later, Oliver and his finance director, James Montague, opened the door from his office and came in, both of them with huge smiles on their faces.

"We've done it Karis! Our offer has been accepted." Oliver's voice was excited and he was obviously feeling very elated and pleased with the outcome of the conference. "It is, of course, subject to some small adjustments, which we expected anyway, but nothing that we can't fix fairly quickly. God! That was hard work!"

Karis jumped to her feet. "Thank God for that! That's really wonderful news, Oliver. Congratulations both of you. You must be feeling very pleased with yourselves and also huge relief too!" She was genuinely pleased for them, as she knew better than anyone just how hard they had worked and how much it meant to them to make a success of the takeover. There was more than kudos involved here – it was a great achievement and a huge step forward for the company.

"I'll be off now then Oliver," James said. "We'll get together first thing in the morning to get things finalised and nicely tied up.   God, it'll be great to go to bed tonight without worrying about some point or another that I think I may have overlooked.   See you both tomorrow," and with a wave of his hand, James opened the door to the corridor and stepped outside.

Oliver sat down wearily in the chair by the window and looked out and Karis, following his gaze, could see that the sunset had silhouetted the leafless trees along the top of the small hill across the road from the office so that they looked like black skeletons against the rose red sky; it was spectacular and Oliver was obviously enjoying the view while still turning things over in his mind.

"So, we've got the verbal OK but we shall have to wait for the written confirmation before we announce the takeover to the workforce and then to the world.   I must say I feel shattered and strangely exhilarated at the same time and, now that it is nearly all over, somewhat deflated as well. How strange is that?"

Oliver looked at Karis. "The thing is, Karis, it's not all over now is it – now the real work begins, this is just the beginning of the next chapter in the life of our company.   We shall have to integrate the two companies and the workforce, there will be new people to get to know as well as new products, new paperwork and administration and there is also the possibility that I shall have to consider some redundancies."   He paused again, his face serious and lost in thought as he considered possible problems to come.   There was a lot to be considered and to be serious about.

Karis looked at him.   His face was still, full of concern thinking of the work ahead. "It may not come to that," she said.   "Don't think negative thoughts

7

tonight, Oliver, just enjoy the moment and give yourself a night off from worrying about the takeover. You can concentrate and tackle the possibility of problems in the morning."

Her feelings for him had gradually changed over the years. Initially, when she had first met him she hadn't much liked him, disliking his apparent cavalier attitude towards everyone and because she didn't know him very well, she didn't understand his apparent disregard for peoples' feelings when he gave them a 'dressing down' for not doing something in quite the way he had told them to or had asked for. He would raise his voice, slightly, while giving them a reprimand, voicing his disdain or displeasure and frightening the life out of them in the process. She had thought, then, that he had been a bit of a bully. But over the years, he had mellowed and he was now much more tolerant and considerate of his employees.

Oliver was a slender man of about 5'11 or so with a good head of straight brown hair, which he kept fashionably cut, and very blue eyes that looked directly at whoever he was speaking to, giving them his full attention. He had a straight nose, a squarish jaw and a thin-lipped mouth that didn't smile enough but was slightly lopsided when it did. Overall, his face was not quite handsome but it was always interesting, as he didn't try to hide his feelings. His voice was deep and clear and he spoke without any discernible accent and he looked honest and without guile, the sort of man you could trust with your life and totally dependable. He was not big boned but his shoulders were broad and powerful, the result of playing a lot of sport and his whole body language suggested that he was a man unafraid of anything.

Karis had been working for him for seven years. She started her employment with him, luckily she now felt, by being in the right place at the right time. Wasn't nearly everything in life about timing? She had thought long and hard about whether she really wanted to take the job when he offered it to her, being comfortable and happy working for the marketing director of the company, but had finally decided that she had nothing to lose and if she didn't like the job she wasn't tied to it for life and could always leave if she wanted to. And there was, of course, the added prestige of working for the top man, not to mention a very healthy increase in her salary which - with having two children, one a teenager and the other ten years old, both of whose needs and wants were constant - would be very welcome. And so, after turning over all the pros and cons in her mind she had accepted the job and had enjoyed nearly every minute of it ever since.

It had proved both a challenge and a huge learning curve. Oliver was so different from anyone else she had worked for before but, as the time went by, she got to know him better and she also began to understand what made him tick and, more importantly, why. His lack of patience was usually born out of frustration, often because people didn't live up to their abilities and were unaware of their own potential; they gave up too easily, or they didn't try hard enough – where was their ambition to succeed? And often he was right, although not always as he sometimes expected more from people who just didn't have more to give.

Having worked for the marketing director in the same company for a few years, Karis had a reasonable knowledge of the whole company; she knew many of the staff and employees in the offices and the factory and she was aware of its strengths and also in some areas, its weaknesses, mostly in the personnel department, where things were constantly changing and could be improved.

The company had almost doubled in size since Oliver had become its CEO because he had given it much more direction and purpose, raising the expectations of the workforce by introducing several new products to their range. He also made sure that everyone working for the company knew the importance their own particular role played in the smooth running of the company and, also, just what was expected of them in fulfilling that role.

Oliver was married to Kate, a very pretty lady who he obviously adored and they had two beautiful daughters, Jane and Sarah. Jane had worked in Research until she married and then had two children, Crispin and Sophie, fairly rapidly and had, since then, devoted herself to being a full-time wife and mother. Sarah had graduated in business studies and now had her own PR business, employing four other people. Oliver had high expectations for their careers and was a little miffed when Jane chose to give it all up for the sake of her family, but his attitude had changed when he fell in love with his grandchildren who quickly earned his devotion as a doting grandfather. He still anticipated that Sarah would do very well with her company and he was pleased that her priorities seemed to be making a success of her career rather than, like Jane, opting for early marriage. Oliver had always kept his distance from the girls' respective jobs and had no obvious influence on their choice of career, although he still gave them the benefit of his advice when he thought they needed it, whether it was asked for or not.

His own career had seen him achieve success with a variety of companies, originally working on the factory floor as a student during the summer vacation when he had learned valuable lessons in man management as well as the process of manufacturing goods from start to finish and then finally reaching the very top at Clover Cosmetics.

Now that he was 'the boss', Oliver made frequent, and unannounced, visits down to the factory, which was situated in a large building directly behind the office block, which was connected by a covered walkway. These unexpected visits at first caused consternation with the supervisors as he was always asking questions that needed positive answers, but it kept all the factory staff on their toes and as he never forgot to praise good work or pass comment on areas where he thought improvement could be made, his visits were looked forward to.

Overall, the Clover Cosmetics factory was run by extremely efficient and enthusiastic people who were happy to follow the strictly laid down 'rules and regulations' of the company, with perhaps just a few small exceptions. Apart from obeying company law it made for a happy workplace where everyone knew precisely what was expected of them and, usually, they did their best to conform. There were perks of the job by way of a subsidised shop and canteen and a monthly small monetary prize for the employee of the month, so it was in the employees own interest to do their jobs as well as they possibly could.

There were a few exceptions, where a few people tried to push the boundaries or who chanced their luck with a short-cut, but they mostly enjoyed what was a relatively well-paid job, both men and women enjoying the work and the company and the environmentally friendly workplace. Not unusually, the company employed a largely female factory workforce, with male workers doing the supervisory jobs, the engineering, portering and fork-lift jobs, although this was gradually changing and, consequently, there was a great deal of good-natured chat between the men and the women, both genders enjoying the friendly banter.

The factory employed enough men to be able to field and run a football team, which made up for its lack of skill with lots of enthusiasm. The team played regular games against similarly placed local factories, loudly supported by their fellow workers with often rude and robust vocal encouragement. Social evenings, run by the Human Resources Department, were held once or twice a year with the objective of giving the workforce a 'thank you' from the company with live music and dancing. Most employees went along to these social events, including all the office staff, most of them enjoying themselves.

An annual cricket match was organised in the summer between the factory staff and the office staff which always created intense rivalry and competitiveness and ensured that everyone played to the very best of their ability to win, each side being noisily supported by their own supporters. After the match finished, regardless of who had won, everyone enjoyed the jokes and leg-pulling that followed, as well as the food and drinks that were supplied by the company to finish off the day. Oliver always took part in the game as he thought it was valuable PR but also, Karis knew, because he rather fancied himself as a batsman and was more than disappointed if he didn't make a good score. He was convinced that getting the whole company together helped to keep loyalty and good relationships going and he was probably right: it certainly didn't do any harm and it was a good way of repaying the workforce for their hard work throughout the year. It was well worth the relatively small monetary cost to the company.

Karis looked at Oliver, his eyes closed, his face still and obviously lost in thought. He looked tired.

"Oliver, can I get you anything before I go? Tea or coffee, or maybe a whisky? I think you've earned yourself a drink. I must get home as soon as I can, though, as it is Joanne's school play tonight and I've promised that I will be there, on pain of death! Otherwise I'd have something with you."

Oliver opened his eyes and smiled at her, his face suddenly animated and happy again. "No thanks, Karis. I'll have a drink with Kate when I get home. I'll give her a surprise and get home a bit earlier tonight. Like you, she has been very patiently putting up with all this overtime we've been doing recently."

He got up from the chair and came over to Karis where she was standing by her desk.

"I hope the play is a huge success, Karis, and I am sure you are looking forward to enjoying an evening of relaxation for a change. Please pass on my congratulations and best wishes to Joanne for me. She has done incredibly well and you must be very proud of her."

And then his face became serious. "I'm very grateful to you Karis. You have been very patient with me and my mood swings while we have been working so hard on this acquisition, never complaining when you had good reason to. Or, come to think about it, all the time I guess," he grinned at her. "You've done a very good job keeping my nose to the grindstone when I wanted to call it a day, staying for lots of late nights and not telling me to 'get lost' when you had very good reason to. You have worked well above and beyond the call of duty and I honestly don't think I could have managed without you. And, while I think of it, please thank Jonathan for me, too, for his understanding as he must have been pretty fed up with all of us just lately while we've been working so hard."

He put out his hand and touched her arm, his eyes searching hers, and then he bent his head and gently kissed her on the cheek.

Chapter 2

Today

Jon turned the key in the lock, pushed the door open and they stepped inside; first impressions were encouraging. For the past several months, Karis and Jonathan had been looking for a house or cottage they could buy and move into which, for financial reasons, had to be fairly small and, at last, maybe they had found one that would tick all their boxes.

Pretentious it certainly wasn't. From the outside, the house was almost exactly like a child's drawing of a house; four windows to the front of the house, with bay windows downstairs, a wooden front door painted in dark green which was enclosed by a small porch which was in the centre of a red brick wall under a grey slate roof. Two chimneys were positioned at each end of the house. A redeeming feature in an otherwise very plain looking building was that a peach coloured rose had scrambled all over the porch and was in profusive full flower, softening the whole plain outline and giving off wafts of a delicious scent.

The small front garden was just that – small, just the width of the house, covered in shingle with a central brick path to the front door and another path going off to the right round to the back of the house. Small flower borders were to each side of the front door under the bay windows and were mostly covered in weeds but with a few neglected perennials showing through in places. A white picket fence was at either side of the garden separating the property from the houses on either side which were similar but not identical in a row of six. All had been built in Victorian times and were in a small cul-de-sac leading off from a side road in a village on the edge of the New Forest. Not having been lived in for over a year, it was dilapidated and run-down.

The accommodation, sounding quite different on the estate agent's leaflet to that which was now in front of them, was literally two up and two down with the sitting room leading off from the small entrance hall to the left and the dining room leading off to the right. Stairs leading straight up were about 5 feet in front of them as they stepped into the hallway, with a very small landing area which led into two bedrooms directly over the sitting and dining rooms and with a central bathroom beyond which had been added on to the original cottage. A kitchen downstairs had also been built on behind the dining room and that had a French window leading out into a small walled garden. A very small cloakroom had been built in what had probably been a pantry originally, in the space under the stairs and this was accessed from the dining room.

Karis stifled a sigh; trying to show some enthusiasm and not her frustration was beginning to be a challenge and she would have to try harder not to lose her patience. The truth was that she didn't want to be looking at another bloody house; she wanted her old one back.

A huge change in their financial circumstances had meant that their income had dramatically dropped a couple of years ago. This was due entirely to a decision that Jonathan had made and it was now necessary that they make savings so that they could survive their resultant straightened circumstances, hence the house-hunting for a small property.

However, there had to be a bright side, didn't there? At least Jamie and Joanne had now left home, although Karis acknowledged that that in itself wasn't necessarily a good thing, but at least they had finished their education and were now both in good jobs and not totally reliant on their parents anymore so Karis and Jon only had themselves to think about.

There was no longer any real need for them to have a four bed-roomed house where a spare bed was always available just in case either Jamie or Joanne decided they wanted to spend a night at home with their parents, often bringing friends along as well to enjoy the hospitality. Now they could easily manage with just one spare bedroom, plus the usual facilities and a small garden but it was proving very difficult to find something that was exactly what they were looking for, particularly in their limited price range.

Karis forced her lips into a smile as she tried to show some enthusiasm. "Nice little entrance – it would look hugely better with a coat of paint although huge is probably not the right word! Minute would be better." She was thinking out loud rather than passing a comment.

As the cottage was so very small, looking over it didn't take very long. Practically every wall in the house was either covered in peeling flowered wallpaper or painted in a variety of colours, mostly in various shades of cream. The woodwork was dull and discoloured with gloss paint no longer glossy and the rooms in comparison with their old house where the ceilings were high and the rooms large, felt terribly small.

However, the sitting-room and dining-room had a little bit more space with the bay windows, and with a smidgen of imagination, Karis felt that the cottage could be made into a home that they could live in. Both the kitchen and the bathroom were in need of some modernisation but Jonathan was a dab hand at DIY and she could paint a bit so between them they could make it habitable and user friendly. At least the little walled garden at the back gave them some scope for creating an extra 'space' which could be made to look very pretty and would, at least, be private, as it was not over-looked. A few climbing plants and some strategically placed tubs with flowering shrubs would improve things instantly.

"What do you think?" Karis asked.

Jonathan looked at her, his eyes, for once, showing a little interest. "It's OK. I guess we could just about manage with just the two of us. Do you think you could cope in the kitchen? It's very small in comparison with our old one; not much room to swing any cats."

Karis smiled at him, reminding herself again that she should try and make an effort to show some enthusiasm. "Good job we haven't got any then, isn't it? It's fine and I think it'll do. Just needs a lick of paint and it'll look quite different." Nothing, she reminded herself, is ever perfect but things could always be improved. "It'll save me having to run around a lot. Who needs an island in the kitchen anyway?"

"OK then. We'll put in an offer as soon as we get home."

As they locked up the house and walked back to the car which was parked down the road, Karis's mind went back over the past few years. They had not been good.

Their problems had probably started when, against her wishes, Jonathan had left his long term job working as an insurance broker. He had joined the company straight from school after taking his A levels and then worked his way up the promotion ladder over a number of years. The job may not have been exciting but it provided steady employment, which he handled with ease and it had paid him a decent salary with prospects of gaining further promotion as the company expanded and he became more proficient and expert in all areas.

And then, out of the blue and completely out of character, he had been talked into taking on a job as the marketing manager for a new company by an old school friend with whom he had maintained close ties since leaving school. The new company made custom built furniture and needed a capable and enthusiastic marketing man, Jonathan, to market the product, find customers and help build the company up. The old school friend, Roger Burgess, had told Jonathan that it couldn't fail but, unfortunately, Roger's skill as a carpenter and his enthusiasm and energy were not matched by his business acumen.

Roger had been left a pot of money by his grandmother and he had decided, after a lot of deliberate thought, to branch out on his own and start his own company instead of working as someone else's 'dogsbody' as he put it. Jonathan had been caught up in his enthusiasm, and feeling bored and somewhat frustrated with his own job, had agreed to join Roger without mentioning it or talking it through with Karis.

For the first few years everything worked out reasonably well. Karis had not tried to hide her disapproval of Jon giving up his job to do something completely new, as she had huge reservations and felt that the change in circumstances obviously carried some risk; he was also giving up a job for life and a good pension at the end of his working life. On the other hand, she didn't want to put too much of a damper on it either as Jonathan obviously enjoyed the new job, learning new skills getting on very well with his colleagues and meeting lots of new and interesting people by way of clients and customers. He was naturally outgoing and friendly and had an easy manner with people, which they liked and which helped to bring in business for the company.

He hadn't enjoyed being tied to a desk and much preferred the freedom his new job gave him to being restricted to office hours and routines. And it also paid him very well.

After Jon had been in his new job for about 18 months or so Karis had given up her job with Clover Cosmetics and taken a part-time job as a volunteer with a local charity. For some time Jonathan had been trying to persuade her to slow down a bit and spend more time at home but she didn't feel ready to give up work completely and, in fact, was reluctant to give up her full-time employment even though Jon's new job and increased salary meant that her contribution to the family income was not as necessary as it had once been, particularly as both Jamie and Joanne had left home so were no longer a drain on their financial resources.

Leaving Clover Cosmetics had been made easier for her as Oliver had decided to retire when he got to his 60th birthday so he could spend more time with Kate and his family. He had talked things over with Karis and confessed that he felt guilty about neglecting them in favour of his job and he felt that he had gone as far as he could with the company anyway and that the time was right for him to go.

Karis was asked to stay on to work for the new CEO which she did for a while but she found that without Oliver in charge, her enthusiasm for the job was no longer there.

The working practices she had been used to and was familiar with had been radically changed by the new incumbent who was obviously intent on making an impression on the company and how things should be done. It wasn't that Karis didn't like him but she missed the friendly familiarity that Oliver had generated and felt that it was time for a new PA to take over.

Jonathan was delighted. He said he wanted her to be able to relax a bit more and take things easy and that he wanted to take care of her.

It was probably a mix of circumstances that brought about a downturn in the fortunes of the new company after just a few years; lack of judgement, poor management of finances, too many employees chasing too few jobs, the stagnant market place and the poor economic outlook probably all contributing to bringing about the failure of the company, compounded by not enough investment in the first place. And also the competition had been fierce and getting new business had proved harder than anticipated. And the timing was wrong.

But it was only when Jon came home one day and announced to Karis with a very solemn face that he had lost his job that Karis had any idea that the company was in serious trouble, as he had behaved, all the time, as if everything was absolutely OK. But worse was to come. Jonathan had been given a lump sum when he had left the insurance company, having worked for them for twenty or so years, plus a small pension which he would be able to draw when he reached 60.

And then he told her that he had been given 'the opportunity' to invest in the new company when he had started working for them, which he had done using their nest egg without either telling her or consulting her and which left Karis, when he at last plucked up courage to tell her, speechless with anger and disbelief. Their entire savings had disappeared down an enormous big black hole forever instead of quietly gaining interest for their future.

The loss of Jon's job and the subsequent downturn in their finances meant they had to sell their lovely old Victorian house, which they had both loved and which they bought soon after they married, Jon's parents having given them a substantial sum of money as a wedding present which they used as their deposit. They still had a large mortgage on it but could no longer afford the repayments.

The house had been built as a family home. It had two big, high-ceilinged reception rooms, both with inglenook style fireplaces which had been converted to wood burning stoves and which they had furnished with huge squashy sofas and chairs in muted greens, bronzes and apricot colours, plus a large refectory style oak dining table and six chairs they were lucky enough to find at a charity shop. There was an Aga in the kitchen that was always warm and cosy and a children's play room leading off from next to an outhouse which they converted into a utility-come-everything room for wellingtons and umbrellas and which defied description - usually called the glory hole - being constantly changed around as successive games and toys took precedence over previous favourites.

The plumbing throughout the house was inclined to be suspect but worked most of the time when encouraged by a strategically placed thump with a rubber mallet and the running of a bath was usually accompanied by various gurgles and slurps and rattles, much to Jamie and Joanne's amusement. The four bedrooms were also large and the house, built in the middle of a corner plot in suburbia, was surrounded by a huge garden full of old fruit trees and flowering shrubs and it even had a vegetable patch tucked away to one side. The whole house and garden was a children's paradise but they all loved living there.

Not for the first time, Karis wondered just how Jonathan could have invested all that money without talking to her about it in the first place; had he realised that she would have said no? The money had been held in a separate account which she never looked at so hadn't noticed anything amiss, using only their joint current account for their household shopping. There was no way that she would ever make that mistake again.

She was sick of going over and over again in her mind what had happened. Hadn't they always solemnly promised each other that they would never, ever take big decisions about their lives together without consulting the other one, and then, against all predictions, Jonathan had done precisely that.

But there was little point in continually crying over spilt milk; the damage had been done. Unfortunately, there was very little likelihood of them ever getting any money back from the investment, except maybe a small amount when the bankruptcy was finalised, so there was absolutely no point at all in constantly going on about it. They had to make the best of a bad job and she would just have to go back to work, which was not a thought that she relished but which she could and would do.

Their problems had got worse, though, when Jon became severely depressed about the situation they found themselves in and, realising that he was the cause of their troubles, he subsequently suffered a nervous breakdown. Realising he had made a mistake, he tried to pretend that it wasn't anything to worry about but the strain of appearing to not worry became too big a burden and he eventually gave up the struggle of trying to be cheerful and normal and started to drink in secret which then, in turn, led him to sitting and staring into the middle distance for long periods of time. Karis did her best to reassure him that they would, somehow, recover but nothing she said convinced him that things would get better again or gave him any comfort.

When he had first lost his job he had appeared to act both rationally and normal but after a few months when he was unable to find another job in spite of attending many interviews, his demeanour became morose and disinterested in doing anything at all; he even found it difficult to get out of bed or to have a normal conversation, talking mostly in mono-syllables.

Karis, in despair and desperate to try to make their situation better, tried to talk to him but he brushed her aside, insisting that he was fine and would find a job eventually. He flatly refused to discuss her suggestion that he should see their doctor, insisting that he was OK and that everything was all right. Without telling him, Karis saw their doctor herself and spoke to him about Jonathan's problem but, as she expected, he said there was nothing he could do to help until Jon came to see him for himself. And that was the way it stayed for several months until one day Jon broke down in tears and when Karis tried to comfort him, said that perhaps it was time to ask the doctor for some medication to help him get better.

The relief Karis felt when Jonathan agreed that he should see a doctor, was tangible, as if a very heavy burden had been lifted from her shoulders and for the first time, tears fell. Together they went to the surgery and saw the doctor who listened carefully and was sympathetic to the problem. He prescribed group therapy and anti-depressants and, after a few meetings with the therapy group, which Jonathan disliked intensely at first, he gradually began to be more tolerant with the other people in his group and to realise that he was far from alone with his problems. And after a few months on his medication, the black mood that had enveloped and stifled him since the loss of his job gradually began to lift and their life together gave some semblance of starting to get back to where it had been before disaster had struck.

Karis hadn't looked seriously for a job during this time as she felt that Jonathan needed her to be near him as he looked to her for re-assurance about virtually everything, having lost all his confidence doing even routine and small chores. However, she was hopeful that having gradually regained a small amount of self-reliance, he would soon be able to cope more on his own and she would be able to go back to work again to earn some much needed money.

They drove home from viewing the house in silence, each lost in their own thoughts. Currently they were renting a small flat while they looked around for somewhere else to live. They had received an offer to buy their old home almost as soon as it had gone on the market, the offer being much too good to turn down and which would enable them to buy a new smaller place without the need to have a mortgage. They had accepted the offer and as the purchaser wanted a quick buy, they had moved out of the house and into the flat in a matter of weeks, putting most of their furniture into store. The flat was an interim arrangement while they looked for a smaller home and maybe, with a little bit of luck, they had, at last, found a house that would meet their needs and particularly their budget. Not having her own furniture and effects around her made Karis feel a bit lost and unsettled, as she was comfortable and happiest with familiar things around her.

After living in the flat for a few months now, it would be good to get settled in a home of their own again with the added feeling of security around them. Now all they needed to help them on their way was for the owners of the cottage to accept their offer.

Chapter 3

Jonathan rang the estate agents as soon as they got back to the flat, putting in an offer, which they had discussed together and thought was reasonable. Although the house was just about habitable, it hadn't been lived in for nearly a year and some money would have to be spent on it to make it liveable in and some way towards what they would like it to be. As it had been empty for so long, some deterioration had taken place and it had an unloved, unlived in feel and become shabby as a result. In other words it was in need of lots of TLC to make it OK to live in and a home again.

"They said they would ring the owners and get back to us as soon as possible." Jon looked at Karis, hoping for her approval, his face still showing signs of anxiety.

Karis looked away, wondering what he was feeling. Even after all this time, in spite of herself, she was still cross with him and she could do without that 'poor little boy' look which used to have the ability to melt her heart but which she now found, much to her surprise, more than mildly irritating. Having to leave their lovely home which she had anticipated they would live in for the rest of their lives together still hurt and it would take her a very long time to get over if, in fact, she ever did.

"Good. I'll get dinner." Karis turned and walked into the kitchen. She had changed into a soft blue jersey leisure suit and, in spite of herself, couldn't help feeling a lift of her spirits. Maybe the new house would give them a fresh start. Jon might find another job- so might she. Lots of mights here, she thought, but also lots of possibilities too! Maybe a new chapter in their lives was beginning. She was surprised to hear herself starting to hum a song.

"Would you like a glass of wine?" Jon asked, coming into the kitchen and going to the fridge.

"Yes, I would," Karis answered quickly. "Let's think positive and assume we are going to have our offer accepted."

They both laughed as Jon opened the fridge door. It had been a long time since they had shared laughter and wine which for most of their life together, had been more usual than not until disaster had overtaken them.

"Red or the other sort?" he asked.

"Red, please, Jon. We've got lamb chops, dauphinoise potatoes and broccoli for supper, which will be ready in about half an hour and, as everyone knows, a glass of wine a day is good for us, particularly red. Not that we need an excuse. We deserve it."

Jon poured the wine, passed a glass to Karis and they clinked glasses, looked each other in the eyes and smiled. The wine, a fruity Merlot tasted wonderful.

They had been in love with each other since they were in their late teens, having met at a school dance and, literally, been inseparable ever since. Everyone at the time, and in particular their parents, had said they were too young to know what they were doing when they said that they wanted to get married and spend the rest of their lives together but they knew, with the certainty and confidence of the young, that the depth of love they felt for each other was more than just a passing fancy; it was very special and they were completely convinced that their mutual love and affection would last forever no matter what life had in store for them.

Karis could remember vividly the first time she saw Jonathan, leaning nonchalantly against the wall, tall and slim with dark blonde straight hair and blue eyes, his mouth curved into a smile as he listened to a friend who was talking to him. And although it wasn't exactly love at first sight she could remember her stomach giving a lurch and thinking 'he looks nice. I wonder if he'll ask me to dance', and her excitement when later on in the evening, he did.

Karis appeared to have lost her power of speech when he took her in his arms and they fox-trotted round the school hall where the dance was being held; she just smiled at him and concentrated on matching her steps to his. It wasn't hard as he was a good dancer. "You dance very well," he said, "Are you with anyone or can I take you home?" It was as simple and as quick as that.

From then on they spent as much time as possible with each other, their friendship gradually turning into love and then commitment. Gradually, their parents came to accept that they were serious in their feelings for each other and eventually agreed and gave them their consent to them getting married on the condition that they should both secure 'proper' jobs before getting engaged.

And now, 28 years later, neither of them had seriously looked at anyone else in all that time, at least not with love. There had been the odd occasion when Karis admitted to herself that there had been one or two men she had fancied, albeit briefly, but it had been no more than that, just a passing fancy and she thought it was more than likely that Jonathan felt exactly the same way as she did. Which, when trying to analyse what had happened to them, made it much harder for her to understand; why had he acted so completely out of character in investing their money without talking to her first about his intentions?

But what was to be gained by being forever angry – more lines on her face and an upset stomach through anxiety! Common sense told her not to go there. She and Jonathan still had years of living in front of them so they might as well forget the past and enjoy the present as much as they could. Even if they lived fairly frugally, they still had the physical pleasure and comfort of each other, plus the added joy of two lovely children.

The chops were grilling nicely and the wine was going down very well, inducing a comfortable warm feeling as it did so. It's the simple things in life one has to be grateful for, Karis thought as she turned the chops over. We're both reasonably healthy, we are lucky to have Jamie and Joanne who are also healthy and doing well for themselves and most of all, in spite of everything that has happened, we really do still love each other.

Karis put the food on the table and finishing her glass of wine said, "That was lovely – let's have another one. Never mind saving some for tomorrow."

They were both beginning to feel relaxed and happy - perhaps their recent unhappy time was on the way to being a thing of the past. Jon playfully tugged at her ear and then kissed her lightly on the lips as he stood up to get them more wine. For a long time now, they had been keeping each other at arm's length, their previous closeness and need for contact having been overtaken by antagonism and a feeling of detachment which both of them hated but which neither felt able to overcome; Jon because he was frightened of annoying her even more than she already was, and Karis because she was still feeling hurt, angry and cross with him and absolutely wretched about their quarrel at the same time and she just wasn't ready to forgive him just yet.

Karis smiled and Jon caught his breath; with her beautiful chestnut coloured hair, which she had recently had cut in a chin length straight bob and with her green eyes sparkling, she looked very pretty and for the thousandth time he thought how lucky he was to have her as his wife.

"Assuming that they accept our offer, we shall have to start thinking about making plans for the move and assessing how much it is all going to cost and whether we shall have any money left once we have done some of the decorating that must be done. There is a lot to think about." Karis had a crease between her brows as she spoke.

"I'd prefer to wait for the OK before we start making plans," Jon said, not anxious to start planning for something that just might not happen.

"That's typical of you," Karis replied. "Wait until the last minute and then do everything all at once in too much of a hurry so that we end up absolutely shattered."

They glared at each other and then burst out laughing.

"Let's not go there, let's just go to bed instead and get a good night's rest in anticipation, perhaps, of some action tomorrow." And with that, Jon took her by the hand and led her into the bedroom.

They lay awake, side by side, not quite touching, each lost in their own thoughts, and then after a little while, Jonathan put his hand on her thigh and gently began to caress her. Karis gave no indication of encouragement but it was a touch that she had missed and it was difficult for her not to be affected by the soothing feeling that his touch generated in her and then, not to respond to the rising feeling of need.

31

Gradually, his hand began to explore her inner thigh and Karis instinctively half-turned towards him as he began to caress her breast. Oh God! She was lost. She turned to face him, her hand going up behind his head to bring his mouth down onto hers. They had made love thousands of times but it was always magic, the primitive urge to become one, unstoppable once they had started to arouse in the other one the need to express their love for each other in physical contact.

After a while, they were both damp from their exertions – tired and exhilarated at the same time.

"What happened to that good night's rest?" asked Karis, smiling in the darkness, her thoughts centred entirely on having both pleased and satisfied her husband as well as feeling totally and completely relaxed in herself.

"We've the rest of the night to sleep and no rush in the morning. I've missed you darling - thanks for coming back to me." Jonathan sighed the sigh of a happy man, turned over onto his side and was asleep in minutes.

Chapter 4

"Good heavens! That can't be the time!" Karis leapt out of bed, throwing the bedclothes over Jon who was still lying bunched up and comatose and obviously still asleep. The hands of the clock showed that it was 8.30 am.

"Where's the fire? There's no rush is there?" Jon turned over onto his back, his face still sleepy and his brain confused; he always took longer to come to terms with a new day than his wife. It was just as well that he had never had a job that required him to make an early start in the morning thought Karis as she tied the belt of her dressing gown and went into the kitchen to put the kettle on and start getting breakfast.

She had forgotten that they had gone to bed hurriedly last night but soon remembered when she saw the state of the dinner table and the dirty grill pan and dishes in the sink. Ugh! Not nice. However, not anything to worry about, she thought as she started stacking things in the dishwasher, and it had been worth it anyway. Hopefully, their recent difficulties and differences could now start to be a thing of the past.

It would be so good to have their own home again, she mused to herself as she looked round the kitchen. Although the flat had served its purpose as far as their short let was concerned, she found it completely lacking in character. It had been furnished and decorated by someone who had very different taste to her own, and she found it functional and featureless rather than pretty and practical or, in fact, anything like she would have decorated it herself. Already, in spite of knowing that it still wasn't a 'done deal' she couldn't but help start thinking about possible colour schemes for the new house.

She looked at the walls of the dining-room/kitchen while she sipped her tea, elbows on the table. Painted a bright yellow, it was probably meant to represent sunshine but Karis didn't like it at all, finding it altogether too harsh a shade and with bright blue work-surfaces, supposedly complementing the yellow, she found it was all too much to cope with, particularly first thing in the morning! It surely should be less 'in your face' and a little bit more subtle? However, it wouldn't matter for too much longer now and she could live with it for a little while longer. Hopefully, they would hear from the agents today, hopefully this morning, with good news and then, with luck on their side and keeping everything crossed, the purchase could go ahead and it would be straight forward with no problems to hold things up. They had another two months to run on their lease which should be just about right to finalise all the legal side of the purchase, as there was no chain involved and then, once they were in the house they could get on with the essential and very necessary decorating.

Jonathan appeared in the doorway looking slightly less befuddled with sleep than he had previously, having brushed his teeth and his hair but still, like Karis, in his dressing-gown.

He grinned at her. "Morning, darling. Did you sleep well? I certainly did." Without waiting for an answer he picked up the coffee pot and poured himself a cup.

"Should I ring the agent again do you think?" He paused, looking questioningly at her.

"No, I don't think so. They've hardly had enough time to have had an answer for us yet. We'll just have to

34

be patient and wait a bit longer. Would you like bacon and eggs for breakfast?"

He thought for a moment and then said, "That sounds very tempting but, no, I don't think so. I'll just have cereal, thanks". He opened the cupboard door and after looking to see what was on offer, extracted his chosen breakfast cereal.

Just then the telephone rang and they both jumped up, Jon getting his hands on the phone first. "Hello. Jon Fielden."

Karis watched his face. Was it the agent?

"Oh, hello darling," he said – not the agent then, probably their daughter Joanne, since Jon wasn't in the habit of calling many people darling. "You're up early today. How are you? Are we going to see you soon?" He listened for a minute or two and then said "I'd better hand you over to your mother – look forward to seeing you soon," and with that passed the phone over to Karis.

"Hi Sweetheart! This is unexpected. Is everything OK?" Jo usually spoke to them in the evening or at the weekend, when she was not busy at work.

"Hi Mum. I wondered if it would be OK if I came over to see you and Dad at the weekend. And would it be OK if I brought a friend as well?" Her voice was casual.

"Of course it would. Why not come for lunch on Sunday and, hopefully, by then we'll have some news for you." And, as an afterthought, "Have we met this friend?"

"No. His name is Lee and I know you'll like him. He's still at university, in his fifth year now – he's going to be a doctor but he'll tell you all about it when we see you on Sunday. Be there about 12ish then. Must fly now as I've millions of things to do – love you lots," and she was gone. Joanne always did everything at speed, preferring to run rather than walk.

"Well! What do you think of that?" Karis looked at her husband who had a bemused look on his face. They were well used to having their daughter bring her friends home from school, and then from college; in fact, theirs had often seemed like an extended family with other people's children often staying with them. Since Jamie and Joanne had been in their teens they had been bringing their friends home for 'overnights' as they called them. So what was different about this one? Nothing that Karis could put a finger on but, somewhere along the line, she had picked up an inflexion in Joanne's voice which told her that this one was 'special' in some way. Surely she hadn't met 'the one' already? In Karis's opinion and definitely in Jon's, Joanne was much too young to think of tying herself down just yet.

"Oh it's probably just another one of Joanne's lame ducks," he said. "We shall find out soon enough."

Their daughter was a physiotherapist, newly qualified and working in her first job as a junior in a clinic which took both private and NHS patients and was in a county town about 20 miles away. She had been there for a few months now and loved the work, renting a small flat for herself within five minutes walk of the clinic, where she lived in a minimalist style that suited her uncluttered and busy lifestyle. On average, they saw her about once a month.

"Well, I must get on. A quick shower and tidy around the flat and then, perhaps, we can go shopping to get something for Sunday's lunch. Is that OK with you Jon? And then maybe by the time we go out we'll have heard from the estate agent." Karis gathered up their breakfast dishes, finished loading the dishwasher and then switched it on. Not for the first time she thought how wonderful it was to have modern appliances to help with the chores.

As she disappeared into the bathroom, Jonathan pondered on his daughter's call. Joanne was petite with long blonde hair; her air of vulnerability belied the fact that she was very strong both physically and mentally, adored playing hockey and tennis and viewed life through her own particular brand of rose-coloured glasses. He and Karis had entertained many of Jo's boyfriends but that was just what they were to her – friends! And, frankly, that was the way he would prefer them to stay. She was his little girl and he was not ready to hand her over to any other man for some while yet.

Just then, the phone rang again. Jon picked it up and repeated his name.

"Hello Mr Fielden. This is Jeremy from Aston's the estate agents and it is just a quick call to let you know the good news that the vendors have accepted your offer on the cottage. As you know, it has been on the market for some time now and they are anxious to get things finalised as soon as possible. In order to get the ball rolling quickly, as I am sure you want to, there are a few details we need from you, Solicitors' name, financial details etc. Could you possibly call in this morning so that we can get things moving?"

"That's very good news, Jeremy, and thank you for letting us know quickly – we were wondering if we would hear from you today. Yes, we too, are looking to get the purchase through as quickly as possible and since there is no chain involved and we have the finance available, it should all go through with very little trouble. We could call in to see you with the necessary details in a couple of hours or so. Shall we say 11 o'clock? Is that OK with you? Good. See you then." Jon was smiling as he put the phone down. Karis was going to be so pleased to hear their offer had been accepted.

Just then she came out of the bathroom, wrapped in a huge towel. "Judging by the look on your face, I think we've had some good news. Is it a yes?" Her tone was eager.

"Yes, it's a yes. I've said we'll get in to see them in a couple of hours to give them the various details and bits and pieces that they need to get the ball rolling and we can then go on and do a shop afterwards. Perhaps we can call in and have a drink somewhere as I think we should celebrate. What do you think?"

"I think that's a great idea." Karis smiled at him. Things were definitely getting better all the time. "It also might be a good idea if you have a shave and shower first though, don't you think?"

Ever practical, my wife, Jon thought as, smiling at her, he stooped to kiss her gently on the lips and then made his way to the bathroom, both of them feeling vaguely excited and happier than for a very long time.

Karis dressed carefully, putting on her best black trousers and a cream cashmere polo neck with short black leather boots and a pale blue jacket. The sun was shining and there was some warmth in the March air which, after a long grey seemingly interminable winter, was a change for the better and more than welcome. The rise in her spirits was tangible and she hoped that Jon was feeling exactly the same way.

Looking out of the dining room window, Karis could see a few daffodils about to burst into bloom above the primroses that had been flowering for the past few weeks and were likely to go on flowering for some time yet. This time next year, she thought, if everything works out as we want it to, we shall have some lovely tubs of flowers in our little walled garden, some forsythia and maybe some wall-trained apples and pears and also some climbing roses and clematis. There was a lot to think about, to plan for and to look forward to. She could hardly wait.

They spent longer at the estate agents than they expected to so that when they finally emerged they were more than ready for a drink. Jon tucked Karis's arm through his and they walked quickly to a small, very old pub in the oldest part of town. "What would you like?" he asked as they walked into the bar, "Gin and tonic?"

"No thanks, Jon. I think I'll have half of best bitter. I would expect that they'll have a good one on draught here." Karis smiled at him and then at the barman who was hovering the other side of the bar, waiting for them to give their order. A log fire crackled in the fireplace, reflected in the horse brasses that were hung on either side of the chimney breast on polished leather straps. "Lovely to see a fire, even though it is a nice spring day outside" she said.

She glanced round the bar, noticing the sparkling glasses and the clean polished bar as she did so, as well as which wines were on offer by the glass. Having spent some time in her youth helping out at a very popular pub in her home town, she was well aware just how much hard work went into keeping a busy bar operating as a well-run social meeting place. This one had care written all over it and was definitely a bit special.

Jon ordered himself a pint of the same and they then sat at a small table to discuss the last hour they had spent at the estate agents.

"They seem to be confident that we might be able to wrap things up within a couple of months with the vendor anxious to sell and us ready with the money.

Any longer than that and we could be in trouble with our lease running out on the flat." Jon sipped his beer and then smiled, "Good choice, Karis. That's very nice. Obviously well looked after, the right temperature and clear as a bell," and he raised his glass to his wife. "Here's looking at you," he said, looking quite serious but with smiling eyes, "and I like the view."

Karis smiled back at him and raised her own glass. What a difference a day makes, she thought. Yesterday, I was feeling down in the dumps and fed up and now, one day on and everything had taken a turn for the better. All they needed now was for them both to get decent jobs and they would be on an upward trend again. But they had made a start.

"I think we should be OK. As we all agreed, there are no obvious difficulties with the purchase as we have the money ready and waiting to buy. What could possibly go wrong?" Karis was determined to keep the good feeling alive. She'd had more than enough of feeling that she was at the end of her not unlimited ability to keep cheerful; she much preferred to be positive.

They discussed what they needed to do to tie up the purchase and first and foremost was to contact their solicitor to let him know what was happening. They agreed that Jon would ring him as soon as they got home, although their call was unlikely to be a surprise, as he knew that they had been looking for a suitable new home for some time now. He had handled the sale of their old house so was familiar with their circumstances and well organised with all the necessary paperwork.

"Time to go shopping for some food, I think," said Karis. "What about a leg of delicious Welsh lamb for lunch on Sunday? It's ages since I've cooked one and I think, as this is a special occasion, we can afford to be a bit extravagant."

Both Karis and Jonathan were good cooks, each appreciating the other's culinary skills, often taking it in turns to cook supper in the evening, but over the past year or so while Jon had been ill, Karis had done most of the cooking, producing tasty meals from cheaper cuts of meat or minced beef or pasta as there was not the money available for the more expensive cuts of meat that they were used to and which they preferred. And Jonathan's depression had meant that he just hadn't wanted to do any cooking at all and, in fact, had mostly lost his previous enthusiasm for eating anyway.

"That sounds great to me. Good idea, Karis." Jonathan said. "And we'll have a decent bottle of red to go with it; how to win over and, maybe, influence Joanne's friend. I shall enjoy it even if he doesn't."

Golly! That's a change for the good, Karis thought, some enthusiasm at last. Let's hope we can keep that going.

Separately, they both wondered again what sort of man Lee was and whether they would like him and whether he would like them. Karis thought it unlikely that Joanne would be bringing him to meet them unless he was a pleasant and civilised character. It would also be good to see Joanne for a little while, too, and hear how she was getting on with her job; telephone calls were fine but it was so much better seeing her in the flesh.

Chapter 5

Karis and Jon were both up early on Sunday morning, eager to get on with preparing lunch. It was a beautiful day; sunny with a clear blue sky, the birds twittering in the trees and flitting about building nests and with a promise in the air that spring always brings. Spring flowers were in full bloom, some shrubs were already flowering and some of the trees around the garden were beginning to show a hint of green as their leaves began to unfurl. The hawthorn in the hedge at the bottom of the garden was already showing signs of producing flower heads with the leaves now fully open.

Jon peeled the potatoes, parsnips and carrots while Karis stuck small pieces of rosemary and garlic into the fleshy parts of the lamb, a companionable togetherness between them. Karis was planning for lunch at 1.30ish, which would give them time to have coffee and then a drink before lunch while they caught up with Joanne's news and made Lee feel at home.

"What's for pudding, Ma?" Jon asked.

Karis grinned at him. "I thought we'd have one of M&S's finest with ice cream. There is one in the freezer all ready for us, just waiting to be thawed out. A lovely apricot and almond tart. Will that do?"

"Yes, it certainly will. I'll get it out now so it has time to come up to room temperature."

"I think everything is ready now. We can sit down for half an hour, relax and read the paper before they arrive." Karis was clearly anxious that everything should be right and that Joanne would have a Sunday lunch at home which met her expectations. Jonathan laid the table with a green cloth under a lace top, with a bowl of yellow forsythia and narcissi in the centre, the wine glasses polished and sparkling. It looked very fresh and Karis was pleased with the effect.

It was with lovely, juicy, meaty Sunday lunch smells emanating from the kitchen that Joanne arrived just after 12 o'clock, driving up to the flat in an old, slightly the worse for wear Mini which was the first car she had owned and which was also her pride and joy. Hearing the sound of the car and the noise of two doors being banged shut, both Karis and Jon jumped up and looked out of the window.

Their daughter's face was wreathed in a huge smile, her long fair hair caught up in a ponytail and she was wearing a striped navy and white tee shirt under a light navy fleece and leisure trousers with the inevitable trainers on her feet. She looked fit and very happy. And there was Lee, walking behind her, tall, over six feet, with blond straight hair and gold rimmed sun glasses and a face that was tanned and very serious. Poor man, thought Karis, probably a bit anxious about meeting us; I wonder what Joanne has told him about us?

"Hi darling," she said as she opened the door and clasped her daughter to her in a bear hug, their usual way of greeting each other. "It's lovely to see you. Hello Lee. How nice to meet you," and she shook his extended hand and smiled at him.

He smiled back. "Nice to meet you too," he said and then, turning to Jonathan, shook his hand.

"Come in and I'll get coffee for us all; I expect you could do with a drink after your drive, even though it is not far to come," and not waiting for a reply, Karis disappeared into the kitchen, leaving Jonathan to get his daughter and her friend comfortably seated.

"Traffic not a problem? You've obviously made good time. And you're looking very fit Joanne – obviously the job is suiting you very well."

"I'd forgotten just how small this flat is, Dad. How on earth do you and Mum manage not to bump into each other all the time?" She glanced round the room. "No, the traffic wasn't a problem at all, thank goodness and yes, the job is going really well and I am enjoying it very much."

"Can I give you a hand, Mum?" she said, raising her voice so that Karis could hear her.

"No thanks, Jo," Karis said as she came into the room. "It's all done. I had a tray all ready and waiting so just had to pour the water onto the coffee and it's now ready to pour. We've been busy doing the odd chore this morning and getting lunch ready so we haven't stopped. I'm ready for a caffeine livener."

She poured the coffee, handed round the cups and they helped themselves to sugar, milk and biscuits.

There was a small awkward silence before Jonathan said, "We've got some news for you. We've found a new home, put in an offer and I'm pleased to say it's been accepted. We very much hope to move out of here in a couple or so months and into the new place. It's just a small house in a village about ten miles or so from here but we like it and hope you will too. If you go cross-country, it will be about the same distance from you as this place."

"That's good news, Dad. If you two like it then I'm sure I shall too." Joanne said, sipping her coffee. "It won't be as lovely and comfortable as our old house though, will it? Nothing could ever replace that." She smiled at her mother. "Sorry, Mum. I just think it's such a shame that you had to sell the family silver so to speak." She turned to Lee. "You'd have loved it Lee, lots of lovely big rooms and a huge garden where Jamie and I used to play hide-and-seek and have tree-climbing competitions." Her voice was wistful.

Karis's face was serious when she looked at her daughter. "Nothing stays the same forever, Joanne, circumstances change and it was just too big for just the two of us and it cost an arm and a leg to keep it in good decorative order. We wouldn't have sold it if we had thought there was a chance that we could keep it maintained and as it should be but, needs must and I'm sure we'll be very happy in the new place." Her expression told her daughter that she didn't want to discuss it further.

She hadn't told either Jamie or Joanne the true circumstances of their move from the old house, preferring to keep the loss of their nest egg to themselves, and neither did they tell them how seriously ill Jon had been. Obviously both Jamie and Joanne had known that their father had lost his job but were unaware of the full extent of his illness, thinking that he was just suffering from a bout of depression. At the time, Karis had thought that it served no real purpose to cause them undue concern. She didn't know whether she had done the right thing or not but she had followed her instincts and had decided that she wouldn't worry them and there was absolutely nothing they could have done about it anyway.

"That's enough about us. Tell us what has been happening in your world." Karis looked expectantly at Joanne.

"Well," Joanne said, looking pensive, "the job is going really well and I love it and the flat is OK too, very convenient and not much trouble, which suits me fine. We have quite a lot of patients referred to us from the local hospital where Lee is finishing his training.

You tell them Lee," she said, looking at him with an encouraging smile.

So far, apart from greeting them and then drinking his coffee, Lee had said nothing, although he looked reasonably relaxed and happy just to listen in on their chatter. "Which is how we met," he said. "I knew that some patients were referred to Joanne's clinic as a matter of routine by the hospital where I am training and I thought I would go along myself to suss out the amenities when I had a fall playing squash and damaged my shoulder a bit. That's the gist of it anyway. Joanne gave me some treatment and some exercises to do and that's it really. I was impressed by the clinic and I was also impressed with her thorough approach to my problem and I must say she is a very good physiotherapist; she told me I had to say that!" He grinned at Joanne who playfully raised her hand as if to hit him and they all laughed.

"That's reassuring then," Jonathan said with a smile. "An unbiased opinion of your talent and expertise, Joanne."

"Now, how about a glass of wine? Mum has cooked a leg of lamb for lunch so we thought a nice bottle of red would go down well to go with it. OK for you two? I'm assuming you drink wine, Lee?" Jonathan didn't wait for their replies but opened the bottle and started to pour.

"That'll be great, Dad," Joanne replied, "and, yes, Lee does like a glass of wine but I'm driving so I mustn't drink more than one small glass – not being able to drive would be a disaster for me!"

"A toast, I think." Jonathan raised his glass and said, "Here's to health and happiness for us all and if wealth could be thrown in as well, we'd all be very happy!" at which sentiment they all smiled, clinked glasses and sipped the wine.

Lunch was a very happy occasion; the meat was tender, juicy and tasty and the vegetables cooked to perfection. The four of them chatted as they ate their fill and then finished off the pudding as well, the conversation flowing easily between them. Karis felt relieved and happy that everyone had enjoyed the lunch and gradually relaxed as time went on.

"Thanks, Mum, that was really super. It makes a nice change to have a decent lunch instead of my usual Pot Noodle," Joanne said. She laughed and looked at Karis whose face looked horror-stricken. "Don't worry, I'm only pulling your leg. Of course I eat properly, it's just that sometimes I have to have something quickly and often convenience food fits the bill. And anyway, Lee is a very good cook so he often treats me to a nice meal."

Joanne had not been the easiest child to feed and was fairly choosey, not to say, difficult over what she ate. She had always had definite likes and dislikes and was fussy about what she put in her mouth and she always read labels on jars and tins to make sure that she wasn't eating rubbish or too many additives. She looked very fit and well now, though, so was obviously looking after herself properly.

During the afternoon, Lee told Karis and Jon a bit about his background and that he came from Chester where he had been born and grown up. His parents had a sports outfitters shop which they had owned and run together since they married and which they were now thinking of selling so they could take early retirement and then, hopefully, set off to travel the world like a couple of students. It was something they had always wanted to do when they were younger, apparently, but hadn't got around to doing so for various reasons, mainly because Lewis and Lee had been born and they had taken priority over their parents' ambitions as well as everything else. Lee's older brother Lewis lived with his wife, Jasmine and baby girl, Lily, in Liverpool where he worked as a solicitor.

"Unfortunately," Lee said, "as he lives where he does and I live where I do, our paths don't cross very often but, with the wonders of modern technology, we are able to keep in close contact and we keep each other up to date with what is going on in our lives. I think that maybe Mum and Dad thought that one or other of us might have wanted to take on the shop as it has done very well, employs several people and has increased its turnover hugely over the past few years, but we had other ideas about what we wanted to do so they've gone on managing it themselves. I know Mum in particular, though, wants to have more free time and as she has been such tremendous support to Dad all these years, I think that he agrees that it is almost time to call it a day. They are hoping I think, that a bigger company will come in and buy them out."

Both Karis and Jon liked the way that Lee spoke of his parents with candour and also with affection. It was obvious they had a very good relationship with each other and with their two boys which would surely augur well in the event that he and Joanne ever became serious about each other.

The afternoon passed quickly and it seemed to Karis that it was no time at all before Joanne said that she thought they had better be on their way as they both had busy schedules tomorrow.

"Mum, could I have a quick word before we go?" Joanne looked at her mother.

"Of course you can, darling. Come into the kitchen. I have something I thought you might like to take with you for your flat as Dad and I have no further use for it," and they disappeared into the kitchen, chatting as they went.

"What do you think of Lee, Mum?" Joanne whispered, not wanting him to know that she was talking about him.

"I think he is very nice and I am sure Dad does too. He's polite and charming with very good manners but if you like him, then that's all that matters, Jo. Why, are you getting serious? Do you think he is the one?"

"I don't know," she said, looking doubtful. "How do you tell? All I know is that I miss him if I don't see him for a few days. But I was sure that I wouldn't get serious with anyone until I was at least thirty and here I am at just 24 getting all 'unnecessary' over a man."

"Just give it a bit of time, Joanne, and enjoy his company and being together. Que sera, sera. You have time on your side and you really don't want or need to rush into things too quickly."

"No. You're right, of course. It's just that I think he is so delicious, I want to be with him all the time, wrap my arms around him and tell everyone that he is mine so back off and find someone else!" She laughed, her face a picture of happiness. "Anyway, we really must be going now as I have some preparation to do before going into work tomorrow."

They smiled at each other, happy to have shared mother and daughter confidences, and then returned to the living room.

"Did Joanne want the slow cooker?" Jon asked.

Karis looked at him and grinned. "Whoops! Sorry, I forgot all about that. Would you like a spare slow cooker, Joanne? Dad and I have no use for it as we have two and our new house is so small we shall have to cut down on all surplus equipment to be able to fit everything in."

"OK, then. No doubt I can make use of it. Thanks. Perhaps Lee would like to give me some cookery lessons," and she looked expectantly at Lee while sounding less than enthusiastic.

Goodbyes were said, the men shook hands and Lee kissed Karis lightly on the cheek and said how very much he had enjoyed the day with them and then, suddenly, they were gone, Joanne driving her little mini away while waving goodbye out of the window.

Chapter 6

The next few weeks passed by very quickly. The legal proceedings on the purchase of the house were processed with no hold-ups experienced as they had hoped and anticipated, but still much to their relief. And, also, much to her surprise, Karis found that as the days passed quickly by, she was becoming more and more enthusiastic about the move in spite of her general apathy about the state of their lives. At the same time she kept an eye open for likely job opportunities in the local papers. As soon as they were settled in and re-organised with decorating and getting the place habitable and comfortable, she would register with a jobs agency and make getting a job her number one priority. Obviously, there was not going to be enough for her to do all day in the house and garden and now that Jonathan was so much better again, she didn't feel that he would need her to be at home all the time and she felt that a little bit of space between them wouldn't be a bad thing, for either of them. And the extra money would, of course, be very useful as well.

And with a little encouragement from her, she was sure that Jon would do the same although, it had to be said, he was more reluctant to get enthusiastic about possible employment than she was. Obviously, the thought of a full-time job again filled him with unease and his self-esteem was a long way off being back to normal or even halfway towards what it was before his depression had taken over their lives.

Occasionally, she would watch him when he was unaware of her looking at him and the anxiety she could see in his eyes belied the outward cheerfulness and enthusiasm he was trying to portray; he clearly needed more time to regain his confidence to cope with a job. However, he had handled all the paperwork regarding the purchase of the house with his old confidence and he was also determined that he would help with the redecoration where he could so that, overall, Karis was encouraged by the improvement in his health. From a physical point of view he appeared to be very fit indeed, helped by his occasional swimming and their daily walking in the countryside.

And at last they got the completion date and their moving in plans could go ahead. Karis arranged for an extra month's extension on their lease of the flat and then contacted the company that was storing the furniture and arranged for it to be delivered a couple of weeks after completion, thereby giving them enough time to at least paint the walls and woodwork so that it was clean and tidy, though not perhaps quite up to the standard of being exactly how they would like it to be with new washing machine, cooker, etc. However, they could easily manage with their old ones for the time being.

They had a busy, enjoyable time choosing and buying paint and all the necessary paraphernalia that decorating entailed – trays, rollers, brushes etc. and they then set to work to transform the unloved, neglected feel of the house into something fresh and attractive that they could live in with pleasure.

It was very hard work. As most of the ceilings had been papered over, it all had to be stripped off which proved a huge challenge. The walls, too, had to be stripped and Karis and Jonathan ended each day feeling elated at what they had achieved and absolutely exhausted with aching muscles everywhere in their bodies from the sheer physical effort at the same time.

However, after a couple of weeks they had the semblance of a tidy house that they could live in. Their furniture and boxes of china and bits and pieces were delivered and unloaded and Karis and Jon spent some time deciding where it was all going to go, soon discovering that they would have to offload a few more pieces of furniture if they were going to be able to move around the house at all. Selling it, though, didn't seem to be an option as there didn't appear to be a second-hand market for furniture anymore so they ended up by giving it to a re-housing company which helped out with supplying furniture and affects to people who had nothing at all. Both of them were very happy with that.

Eventually, they were content with the way the little house looked – favourite pictures on the walls, cushions and curtains all blending in and adding colour to the neutral scheme and with the essentials in the way of their old white goods all in reasonably good working order in the kitchen. Yes, it wasn't very big and a long way off what they had been used to, but it would be adequate and comfortable and fine for the foreseeable future. Having got the house fit and ready for them to live in, they could now give some attention to the areas outside of the house; Karis, now fired up with enthusiasm, could hardly wait to get started.

They had just finished coffee one morning after they had spent some time in the garden deciding what to do with it when the phone rang.

"Hello. Is that Karis Fielden?"

Karis didn't recognise the voice but agreed that she was.

"Mrs Fielden, I believe that you once worked for Oliver Melrose?"

"Yes, I did," she agreed.

"Well, I am sorry to have to tell you that he died a few days ago. I am his solicitor, Edric Longmore. I believe we may have spoken on the phone while you were still working for him." Without waiting for her answer, he went on, "I understand that you kept in touch with him after leaving his employment and his widow, Kate, told me that she thought that you may wish to attend the funeral."

"Oh dear! How very sad. I am so very sorry to hear that." Karis was taken completely by surprise at the news and promptly sat down on the nearest chair. However, after a moment or two absorbing the news, she quickly recovered from the shock and said, "Yes, of course my husband and I would both like to attend the funeral. Please let me have the details of when and where it will be." Her distress at the news had temporarily knocked her off her efficiency perch but her voice gave no betrayal of the shock she felt. She went on, "The last time I spoke to Oliver, which was a few months ago now, he sounded full of life with no sign of any illness at all. Did he have a heart attack, Mr Longmore?"

"Yes, Mrs Fielden, he did. It was a massive attack that happened without any warning whatsoever, except for a reference to possible indigestion and there was really nothing that anyone could have done to prevent it. Mrs Melrose was assured by the doctor that Oliver didn't suffer. In fact, true to form, he and Kate had just had a family gathering the previous weekend when their two daughters and their families were down from London for the weekend and Oliver seemed absolutely fine then and on very good form."

"What a dreadful shock for Kate. I do hope she is all right. Please convey my sympathy to her and I shall, of course, be dropping her a note." Karis wrote down the time and place of the funeral. "Goodbye, Mr Longmore. Thank you for letting me know. I was very fond of Oliver and will miss him very much."

Karis turned to her husband. "I expect you heard all that?"

"Yes, I did. I'm sorry Karis. He wasn't very old was he? When is the funeral being held?"

"He would have been 68 on his next birthday in a couple of month's time and the funeral is in eight day's time at the crematorium. No. He was absolutely no age at all. How very sad for Kate and the girls." Karis still sat on the chair she had plonked down onto when taking the call, the phone still in her hand and lost in thought. She had spent many years in close proximity with Oliver, so much so that he was like one of her own family and the news of his death was a horrible, unwelcome shock.

Jonathan had not known Oliver well, having met him on only a few occasions, usually when spouses had been asked along to an official function of the company so, apart from exchanging a few impersonal words, they had not spoken at any great length and then only in polite conversation. He had, though, met Kate on one of these occasions and had spent some while chatting to her and he had told Karis afterwards that he thought that she was a very attractive woman. They probably felt like kindred spirits Karis thought at the time, both being semi-detached from the company. She also got the feeling that Jon had not particularly liked Oliver and she wondered whether she had imagined it or not but the feeling had persisted, maybe because Jon might have felt that she gave her job as Oliver's PA priority over other things – himself maybe - which he considered to be more important. Jonathan was very much of the 'old school' and couldn't help thinking in the old fashioned way that a woman's primary function was to be in the home looking after her family and, not least, her husband! No amount of arguing between them could persuade him to bring his thinking up-to-date and into the real world.

"I'll pop down to the village shop now and see if I can get a card so that I can get it off to Kate today. She must be feeling absolutely shattered, poor girl. I do hope one or other of the girls is staying with her." Karis collected her handbag and her coat from the hall and, calling out to Jon that she wouldn't be long, was out of the door before he could reply.

He watched her as she walked down the road, realising that she was upset but he didn't think she was particularly distressed. Not knowing Oliver that well, it hadn't upset him to hear of his death but he could understand Karis being concerned for Kate and her daughters and wanting to let them know that she was thinking of them. However, since they had had little contact with Oliver since Karis had left his employ, the news wouldn't change their lives at all, and with that thought he went into the kitchen to see what there was for lunch.

Chapter 7

The day of the funeral dawned grey and cold. Karis looked out of the bedroom window with apprehension and a sense of deep foreboding at what the day ahead held for her. First things first though; she had to decide what to wear. She rifled through her wardrobe wondering what she had that would be suitable. She didn't want to wear all black as she didn't think that Oliver would appreciate that but obviously something fairly sombre, reflecting the occasion. She finally selected a pearl grey coloured two piece skirt suit with white blouse and black accessories. "Do you think this is suitable, Jon?" she asked as he wandered into the bedroom.

He looked at the clothes she had in her hands and said he thought they would be fine. He had chosen to wear a dark grey suit himself with white shirt and black tie.

"You look very handsome, darling," Karis said when they were both dressed and ready to go. "It makes a nice change to see you in a suit. Pity it is for such a sad occasion."

They drove to the crematorium in near silence. What was there to say? Karis had lost a friend who Jon barely knew so for him he was just in a supporting role whereas Karis was feeling empty and incredibly sad and lost. She couldn't get her head round the fact that she would never see Oliver or hear his voice ever again and it was causing her real grief and sorrow. Why, she asked herself, hadn't she thought to tell him and to let him know how much she valued and enjoyed his friendship when he was alive? It was too late now.

There were already several mourners at the crematorium when they arrived, some of whom Karis recognised. There were old business associates and friends of Oliver who smiled at her in recognition as well as several unknown faces; they were all looking very serious and solemn. She and Jon stood together at the side of the room where all the mourners were waiting for the hearse to arrive, a quiet expectant hush filling the air. The years since the time when she worked for Oliver and knew his business friends was now melting away to nothing. What a great time she had then and what a marvellous experience it had been. She felt that she had learned a huge amount, about everything, and also experienced a real growing up period in her life.

Sir Hugo Smith was standing nearby and on seeing her, he came over to her and took her hand and squeezed it while kissing her lightly on the cheek, his wife standing by his side smiling gently at her. Sir Hugo was obviously in shock at losing one of his best friends 'before his time'. "You'll miss him as much as I will, I expect," he said, their mutual sadness a bond between them.

The hearse arrived exactly on time and there was complete silence from the mourners as the coffin was carried into the crematorium to the glorious music of Mozart. Kate, dressed in a grey flannel skirt and pale grey shirt under a lavender coloured jacket, was hatless and looking very pale but she appeared to have her emotions well under control. She followed the coffin, flanked on either side by her two daughters, Jane and Sarah. Jane's husband, Tom and their two children, a teenage solemn looking Crispin and his sister Sophie, barely able to contain her tears, walked just behind. Karis caught her breath feeling a lump in her throat from the threatened onset of tears and she discreetly blew her nose as she and Jonathan took their seats towards the back of the crematorium.

Karis looked at the order of service which had a lovely smiley photograph of Oliver on the front, reminding her and everyone there what a good-looking man he had been. It was also fairly obvious that he had been involved in planning the order of service which in between the readings was full of beautiful music which he had loved.

After the service, which had been a sad but at the same time a joyful celebration of Oliver's life and which included a eulogy by Tom that was as good as Karis could have hoped for, Karis and Jonathan were standing outside the crematorium not wishing to be seen to leave too soon, when they were approached by a smallish man with very neatly brushed thinning grey hair; he, too, was wearing a dark grey suit. He introduced himself as Edric Longmore.

"How do you do, Mrs Fielden?" he said, holding out his hand to shake hers and then Jon's. "We spoke on the telephone recently. Mrs Melrose has asked me to invite you and your husband to the wake which is being held at the hotel in the village. I do hope that you can join us?"

Karis looked at Jon. She hadn't expected this and she could tell from his face that he was not particularly in favour of going. "Would you rather not?" she asked and was not exactly surprised when he said that it was up to her whether they went or not.

Making up her mind quickly, she turned to Edric and said that they would be pleased to go, hoping that she wouldn't have cause to regret her decision. After all, what else could she say? She could hardly refuse without appearing to be rude and unfeeling, having specifically been asked to go by Kate.

It took them about fifteen minutes to drive to the village where Oliver had lived with Kate and again there was silence in the car, Karis deciding not to speak as she didn't want to provoke Jonathan into saying that he wished they hadn't agreed to go.

Kate, with her daughters still on either side of her, was standing just inside the room where the food and drinks were to be served, waiting to greet Oliver's mourners; in the circumstances she looked remarkably composed.

"Karis. I am so pleased that you and Jonathan were able to come today. Oliver was so fond of you," her voice sounded cool but polite, matching the expression in her eyes. "I think you will know several old business friends of Oliver's and you know Jane and Sarah, of course." She indicated her daughters, both of whom were looking very solemn and not particularly friendly, which Karis put down to the sadness of the occasion. "And thank you for your kind condolences and card." Her voice trailed off as she turned to greet the next guests coming in the door.

Jonathan accepted a glass of wine from a waitress and also took one for Karis and they then moved further into the room. He started talking to a couple who looked vaguely familiar, exchanging small talk and informing each other where they lived and how far they had travelled etc. making the sort of noises that people make when they know that they are unlikely to see each other ever again. The room quickly became fairly full and the noise levels increased, even though the conversation was muted, as people circulated and chatted to each other. Trays of canapés were being offered and Jonathan helped himself to several but Karis didn't feel in the slightest bit hungry so declined when offered. She did, though, have another glass of wine as her spirits were very downcast and she felt like she needed some alcoholic help to keep her going for a little while longer before they could discreetly disappear.

She chatted to some of Oliver's friends, including Sir Hugo again who, as she had surmised, was feeling very down with the loss of his friend and she also talked to Oliver's grandchildren who were being remarkably stoic in the circumstances. Oliver had thought the world of them and had loved to spoil them at birthdays and at Christmas, giving them inappropriate and extravagant presents that he would have liked to have had himself, and clearly they had loved hearing all about the many adventures he had had as a young man. They both confessed to Karis that they were going to miss him a great deal but Sophie was no longer tearful, having recovered her composure and was looking remarkably pretty, and very like her grandmother, Karis thought.

The strain of keeping her composure was beginning to take its toll on her so after a while and more than enough small talk she was just about to find Jonathan and say that it was time they left when Edric Longmore came up to her and said that he would like a quick word with her before she left. He was looking very serious and Karis had a momentary inward smile to herself as she wondered whether he ever looked anything other than solemn, even when he wasn't being a solicitor.

"Mrs Fielden," he started, "as you know, I was Oliver's solicitor and it is within my duties to administer his estate. Having worked for him for a considerable time you will have a fair idea of what the estate is worth with properties, shares, etcetera, but he was a shrewd investor and he continued to prosper after he left Clover Cosmetics and he was a very wealthy man. What you will probably not know is that you are a beneficiary in his Will and after his family is formally informed of its contents, I shall be in contact with you with details of your legacy."

Karis stared at him. "Are you sure?" she asked, realising as she did so that it was a stupid question. Of course he was sure. "I mean, I had no idea. We were very good friends, of course, but I was only doing my job after all." Her voice trailed off, her mind lost in thought. She was sure that Oliver had never mentioned anything to her about what would happen after he died and certainly never anything about a legacy for her.

Edric smiled. "I shall be in touch shortly. It has been very nice to meet you, Mrs Fielden," and with that he turned on his heel and moved on to another group of people. Were they going to get some news similar to hers she wondered.

The drive home was uneventful, Jonathan again taking the wheel. They were both quiet, lost in their own thoughts on the events of the day. "Thank you for coming with me, darling," Karis said eventually. "I don't think I could have managed it on my own. I thought it went very well, though, and the service was lovely, if ever a funeral service can be lovely. And I think that Kate and Jane and Sarah bore up remarkably well, don't you?"

In fact, going over the events of the day in her mind, Karis felt that Kate's manner had been quite detached and cold but that, surely, was because of the ordeal of coping with everything that the day meant she had to endure and was probably just a front to present to the world. It couldn't have been anything else could it? Did she know about the legacy to Karis? That was nonsense of course as it wasn't likely to amount to very much anyway, just a small token of his appreciation of her work for him and it was likely, she thought, he would have left several legacies of a similar nature surely?

Karis had not mentioned her conversation with Edric to Jonathan deciding that it would probably be better to leave it until she received the promised letter which would then explain things and, hopefully, be a nice surprise for him. Until the letter arrived, she would put it to the back of her mind, although obviously they could do with a helping hand at the moment, even if it was only a few hundred pounds or so, the thought of which brought her back to the present and reminded her that tomorrow she would start some serious job hunting and she would also try and get Jon to do the same.

Chapter 8

The next day was clear and bright in contrast to the previous day and just the sort of day to get things done, Karis thought as she dressed, her thoughts still lingering on yesterday and wondering how Kate was feeling today. She had understood from snippets of conversation she had heard that Sarah was staying with her mother for the time being so that would be company and some comfort for her, and she was likely to be in need of some help with the necessary paperwork that would be coming her way, too. Then what would she do? Karis tried to think from the time when she worked for Oliver what he had said about Kate at home but for the life of her she couldn't remember anything of any relevance. Surely she had plenty of friends who lived locally and who would be making sure that she was not left to spend too much time on her own. Karis thought about what she would do if anything happened to Jonathan and decided that work would be the answer for her, although God forbid anything like that happening for years and years yet.

Her mind roamed over the time she had spent working for Oliver and of her special relationship with him. He had enriched her life with his joy of living, his breadth of knowledge about, she felt, absolutely everything, passing on his enthusiasm to her even if that was not what he intended to do. He had adored his wife and daughters and their welfare was given priority above all things, even the business to which he gave his considerable experience and care, jealously guarding its position in the business world and doing everything he possibly could to make it successful and profitable .

How strange that she hadn't thought much about him or the company since she had left her job. And then, ruefully smiling to herself when she remembered the numerous traumas and dramas and last-minute crises she had coped with while working for him and which, at the time, had taken all her strength both mentally and physically to cope with, it really wasn't strange at all.

Well, at least things had evened out a bit again now and although life had radically changed for her and Jonathan and their relationship had undergone a remedial re-think, at least they were still together and they had a home, although not the one they would have preferred, but a home, nevertheless.

Having dressed in a smart green trouser suit – thank goodness she had kept some of her business clothes – and carefully done her make-up, Karis went down to the living room where Jon was reading the newspaper he had bought from the village shop. He glanced up when she came into the room. "You look nice. Are you going out?"

"I thought I'd go into town, register with one of the agencies and see what the job situation is like. It's time that we both got ourselves employed again," emphasising the both, "as we are going to be short of money any time soon if we don't do something to boost the bank account."

Jonathan looked a little put out. "You didn't say anything about this yesterday," he said, adopting a hurt expression. "I'm not in the right frame of mind to go off looking for a job today," and with that he turned back to the paper.

"OK. That's fine. But I am. I shouldn't be gone too long. I'll get the bus into town and be back as soon as I can. If I'm not back here for lunch, there's plenty of things you can help yourself to in the fridge," and with that she gave him a kiss on his cheek and walked out of the door with a determined step.

I hope he's not going to lapse back into a state of apathy, Karis thought as she walked to the bus stop. He had been quite seriously depressed for a number of months and she was well aware that the recovery period had been protracted and painful for him – for them both in fact. She had tried hard to imagine just what it was like to feel that it was an impossibility to rouse yourself enough to even get out of bed and get dressed, let alone do anything positive but it was difficult, particularly as she had such a delight in living herself. She knew that it was not the thing to do to tell him to 'pull himself together' as the problem went much deeper than that, the mental confusion and inability to want to do anything affecting his physical well being. And so the vicious circle went on and on. No physical exercise equalled no feel-good factor equalled stalemate.

Jonathan had been prescribed therapy and medication and he hated both; the therapy seemed to cause him more problems than he had to start with as he was reluctant to concede that he had any problems in the first place and he viewed others involved in the therapy sessions with a great deal of disdain saying that they had nothing wrong with them anyway and neither had he. And the pills, which he took reluctantly, had taken some time to work and even then, Karis suspected that he often neglected to take them anyway so his progress towards feeling better had been painfully slow.

Karis sighed. She had thought that with the move into the new home and getting settled again and with their relationship regaining some of its old warmth, this would naturally have a positive effect on them both. It had on her but not, apparently, on Jon who remained mostly unresponsive and downbeat.

She was still pondering the problem and hoping that Jonathan would be OK at home when she arrived at the entrance to the agency she had decided to call on first so she put Jonathan and their problems out of her mind and concentrated on what she had come to town for.

A door with the agency name on it was to the side of a small, smart fashion boutique and pushing it open, Karis saw a staircase in front of her and a sign pointing up the stairs.

The office of the agency, after the dimness of the stairs, was full of light. Two girls, practically identical with long blonde straight hair and both wearing sweaters and tight black trousers, were sitting at desks in front of computers with a closed door to one side of the room. A row of filing cabinets were stood against one wall and several big indoor plants were dotted about the room – real not artificial Karis noted with surprise.

"Good morning," one of the girls said as she rose from her desk. "Can I help you?"

Karis told her who she was and said that she was looking for a part-time job initially with a view to possibly working full-time in a few months time. She gave the girl a brief outline of her CV as she handed her a printed copy and noticed the girl's eyebrows shooting skywards when she read the first part of the CV which covered her job working for Oliver.

"I'm sure that Mrs Kerr, the owner of the agency, would like to meet you. I'll just see if she can see you now. Please take a seat." And with that she went to the closed door, knocked and went in closing the door behind her.

Karis was only kept waiting for a minute or two and before she had had a chance to pick up a magazine the girl came back out and said that Mrs Kerr would be pleased to meet her and would she please come in.

Mrs Kerr stood up and held out her hand to Karis. She was about 5'8", with dark blonde hair swept into a French pleat, a smooth white brow and hazel eyes. She was wearing a navy blue two piece, looked super efficient and also very friendly. She was smiling as she said that she was very pleased to meet Karis, please call me Karen and please take a seat. Karis liked her friendly manner and her spirits lifted.

"Thank you for coming to see us, Karis. Judging from reading what you did at your last job I have to say straight away that we haven't got anything at all at the moment at that sort of standard to offer you, although we might be able to find something as you are only looking for part-time work at present. When would you be able to start?"

Karis said that she was thinking about possibly the beginning of next month, which was in just over two weeks time. "I'm not looking for anything high-powered," she laughed; "I've done that. Just something that requires a little bit of intelligence, and possibly some organisational skills. And I realise that technology has moved on since I was last at work over seven years ago now and that my computer knowledge may need some updating. Obviously my last job required spread sheets, presentations and the like but technology being what it is, no sooner do you learn how to use a new application than another one is on the market and you have to start moving on and learning new skills all over again. I do have my own computer at home but, needless to say, I only use it for business letters and keeping in touch with friends via e-mails."

Karen Kerr smiled. "I'm sure you could cope with most jobs having seen what your last employment entailed."

She turned to her computer, hit a few buttons and then scrolled up and down for a few seconds.

"We have a request for a secretary/administration assistant for three days a week at a hospital not far from where you live – it is a special needs hospital - organising the diaries of the medical staff, typing up reports and generally organising things so that they run smoothly. The pay is not great but is that something that you think might be of interest to you?"

"Yes, it is. In fact it sounds ideal, although I don't know much about the medical world. Would that be a problem?"

"No. I'm sure it wouldn't. Shall I make an appointment for you to go and see them and you will then have a better idea what is expected of you."

"Yes please. That would be great. More or less any day would be OK for me."

"I'll ring them now." Karen picked up the phone, punched in the numbers and was very soon talking to the hospital in question. After a conversation which was brief and to the point, Karen put her hand over the mouthpiece of the phone and asked Karis if next Wednesday at 2pm would be OK for her for an interview.

"Yes. That's fine. I just need directions on how to get there and which department I shall be looking for."

Karen asked the necessary questions, made a note on her pad and finished the conversation.

"They'd be very pleased to see you," she said and proceeded to make her notes clearer before passing them over to Karis. "Of course, subject to you taking the job, there will be a contract with us for you to sign as we shall be employing you and paying your salary. Ordinarily, we would ask you to do a written test but I think that in this particular instance we can assume that you are competent in all the necessary skills required for the job so we will by-pass that."

"Thank you." Karis smiled. "I'll let you know how I get on as soon as I know myself." And with that she got up from her chair and extended her hand. "Goodbye, Karen and thank you so much for your help."

Her spirits were high as she stepped onto the street, nearly bumping into a passer-by as her mind was busy thinking of the possibility of a new job. Would Jon be pleased?

Having decided that she would celebrate with a coffee, she made her way to the nearest department store, which had a small restaurant on the first floor. She ordered a cappuccino and sat at a table in the window over-looking the park and was lost in her thoughts about the possibility of a job when she heard her name being spoken. She looked up and was delighted to see the familiar face of a girl who, last time she saw her, was working for the Strategic Planning Department of Clover Cosmetics.

"Helen! How lovely to see you. Are you on your own? Can you join me?" The words tumbled over each other as she thought what a pleasant surprise it was to see a familiar and friendly face. Since Jon's illness, she had more or less lost touch with most of her old friends, only spasmodically seeing a few who were particularly close to her.

"Yes I am on my own and yes, I'd love to join you," and with that Helen pulled out a chair and sat down. "How long is it since we last met? It must be three or four years at least!"

"I don't know, but it's far too long. How have you been and how is Barry?" As Karis spoke she remembered that Helen had had a fairly volatile relationship with her husband, that it had been very much an up and down marriage and she also remembered that there had been rumours at one time that Helen and the finance director were enjoying rather more than a platonic friendship. Better think about what I am saying she reminded herself. "Are you still working or, like me at the moment, enjoying having a lazy time?"

"I'm still working, although not for the same company. Barry and I divorced a couple of years ago and I am now freelance doing contract work. Our financial settlement gave me the house but it was too big for me on my own so I sold up and bought a flat which is altogether more me. And Barry more or less immediately after our divorce became final, started seeing and has now married a girl he knew from his school days. Good luck to them – I am well rid. Her voice was not bitter and her brown eyes were not in the least sad. In fact, with her soft brown curly hair, brown eyes and clear complexion, she looked a picture of health and happiness.

Helen ordered a coffee, stirred in two lumps of brown sugar and then looked enquiringly at Karis. "I heard on the grapevine that Oliver had died. You knew of course?" Before waiting for confirmation or an answer she went on, "Tom Smithson told me when I bumped into him a few days ago. He was one of Oliver's many accountants in case you'd forgotten and he'd heard the news from Oliver's old chauffeur, Bill – remember him? Oliver had a heart attack I believe. You must be quite upset as you two were so close and such good friends."

Karis was surprised by Helen's words. Was she inferring that there had been something between Oliver and her? She searched her face for any sign of malice but there wasn't any. Had other people in the company had the same thoughts?

"Yes, I knew. In fact Jon and I went to Oliver's funeral yesterday. It was all very sad as his death was totally unexpected. I believe it was announced in the national press but, somehow, I managed to miss it. Edric Longmore, Oliver's solicitor, rang and told me the news last week."

"Was there anyone from the company there?" Helen asked. "And how was Oliver's wife?"

"There were a few and Kate, with their two daughters Jane and Sarah, was very much under control." Karis didn't feel like elaborating and decided to keep her comments to a minimum but this seemed to satisfy Helen anyway as she then went on to chat amusingly about various people from the company that they had both known, often making Karis laugh while she did so and bringing back happy memories.

Karis found Helen's company and chatter entertaining and the time flew by. "I really must be going Helen," she said, suddenly noticing that the clock was telling her it was 12.30. "Jon will be wondering where I've got to. It's been great seeing you and I am so glad you are happy and having fun. I have an interview for a part-time job next week and, with a bit of luck, I shall be getting back into the work routine again soon. Seeing you again has made me realise that I've missed the company and friendship of my old work colleagues." She paused before adding, "Jonathan had a nervous breakdown a few years after I left work, so he has been my priority for the last couple of years since then. Fortunately, he is nearly a hundred percent better again now and I'm hoping we can get back to a more normal lifestyle soon. It's been a worrying time."

She wasn't sure whether it was a good idea to tell Helen about Jon as she hadn't broadcast his illness when it had occurred and she had been too preoccupied coping with it afterwards to tell everyone. She had felt it was very much a personal problem and she wanted to keep it quiet while Jonathan recovered.

"No, I didn't know. I'm so sorry Karis but glad to hear that things are better for you now. Good luck with the new job." Helen bent forward and kissed Karis lightly on the cheek. "Hopefully, we can keep in touch with each other now we've met up again. It's been great fun seeing you. Here's my telephone number so please give me a ring sometime and then we can meet for lunch one day. I'd like that," and then she was gone.

It took Karis nearly an hour to get home and she was slightly apprehensive when she opened the door of the house; what sort of mood would Jon be in? She didn't often leave him on his own, or at least only for an hour or so, and this time she had been out for the whole morning. Since his illness, he had become very dependent on her and she worried about whether he would ever recover the necessary confidence to be able to function normally, let alone get another job. His ability to do a good job when fit, she knew, was not in question but it takes more than ability to do a job competently; interacting and getting on with colleagues was also a necessary prerequisite and he was often very 'touchy'.

She needn't have worried. "Hello, darling," Jon greeted her. "I've made some sandwiches and I thought we'd have some soup to go with them for lunch. Is that all right?"

"That's fine, Jon. I'm sorry I am later than planned, but I bumped into an old friend from work and we had a coffee and a gossip together. She had heard about Oliver on the grapevine so of course she wanted to know about the funeral." Karis frowned as she remembered Helen's reference to Karis being close to Oliver, not unreasonable she supposed, given people's liking for gossip.

"And guess what? I've got an interview for a part-time job next Wednesday at the local special needs hospital, three days a week and possibly a whole new learning curve regarding medical language, but I expect I can manage that as there are bound to be reference books around." She smiled at Jon as he passed her a sandwich. "What do you think?"

"That sounds like it will suit you down to the ground. I'm sure you can cope with a new language and as it is not too far away from here, that is another plus. It all adds up to good news and I'm very pleased for you."

"Have you thought any more about trying an agency for a job for you?" Karis asked tentatively, not wanting him to feel that she was putting him under pressure.

"Not really. I was thinking about it this morning while you were out. I'm not quite there yet, and there doesn't seem to be much on the market at the moment anyway. I've looked in the local papers but nothing exactly leapt out at me." He drank some soup and then bit into another sandwich as if it required all his concentration.

"Well, if I get this job, it will help out with the finances and I guess there isn't too much of a hurry for you to get a job as well. I just thought it might be good for you to have something to think about and do; I don't want you getting worried and fed up again. There isn't going to be too much for us to do in the house now that it is all newly decorated, and the garden will more or less take care of itself anyway. But neither do I want you to do anything you don't feel happy and comfortable with. But apart from reading the paper and getting some exercise, I think you are going to need something else to interest you in your life." Jon was looking at the carpet, clearly not happy with the way the conversation was going.

Karis decided that she had said enough. Jon obviously knew how he felt and she must not push him too hard. "Lovely sandwiches, darling," she said. "It was thoughtful of you to make them for us." And then, thinking that she sounded as if she was patronising him, "How about a walk in the forest this afternoon? It's a lovely day, the exercise will be good for us and it will give us a visual and spiritual lift to commune with nature for an hour or two. Good idea?"

"Good idea," he echoed, "but we'll need our boots on today as the recent rain will have caused problems with the paths and they are likely to be muddy." He whistled quietly to himself as he got up to go to the cupboard to get his coat and boots on, glad to have a change of subject.

Chapter 9

The following day was again bright and clear and Karis was opening the upstairs windows when she heard the postman push the post through the letterbox. She had been going through her wardrobe for suitable working clothes and was satisfied that she had enough to be going on with and didn't need to buy anything new when Jon called up the stairs to say that he had made coffee. "Great. I'll be right down."

Jon passed her a cup of coffee and said that there were two letters for her on the table. "Only brochures for me, though, mostly selling aids for the elderly!" He pulled a face. "Absolutely nothing interesting at all for me there, or at least not yet." He picked up his cup and went to sit in the sitting room.

Karis picked up the first letter, and recognising the writing as that of her old school friend Della, she put it on the table to read later. The other was typewritten and she turned it over to see whether it gave any indication on the back who it was from, thinking as she did so that that was a waste of time and it would be quicker to slit it open and find out, which she then did.

It was from a firm of solicitors and Karis noticed the name Edric Longmore in the list of members of the firm at the top right hand side of the letter. She quickly scanned down through the paragraphs as she realised that it was to do with the legacy that Edric had told her that Oliver had left her; her hands were shaking slightly. It was in the third paragraph that she came to the line which said "........the sum of one hundred thousand pounds to Karis Fielden for her friendship, help and loyal support to me in my working life over a period of many years." Karis felt her knees buckling and she quickly sat down on the nearest kitchen chair.

One hundred thousand pounds! Good God! An absolute fortune. Surely there must be some mistake, and she started to read the letter through again to make sure she had read it correctly. Was it in trust? Was it to be shared? Her head was in such a daze that she was not quite able to make sense of it all.

"Are you OK?" Jon appeared in the doorway looking concerned. "You are as white as a sheet. What's the matter? Has anything terrible happened?"

Karis handed him the letter and said, "No, not terrible at all. Quite the reverse in fact. You had better read it for yourself."

He quickly read the letter and, like Karis, read it through again, his eyebrows shooting up his forehead. "Jesus Christ, Karis! What an absolutely fantastic, marvellous surprise." He had a broad smile on his face. "What an incredible reward for typing a few letters." His face was animated, smiling broadly and then, looking at Karis still sitting dumbfounded, asked her if she had had any idea that this was going to happen.

"No. Of course not! I had absolutely no idea at all. And incidentally, I think I did rather more than type a few letters!" she sounded indignant. "Edric Longmore told me at the funeral that I was due for a legacy but I thought a thousand or so at the most. I had no idea it was going to be so much." Karis stared at the letter again, still unable to fully take in what this would mean to them - money in the bank and not having to live hand-to-mouth day in day out. And then another thought occurred to her; Kate had been distinctly cool in her manner to her at the funeral. Had she known then when she saw her how much Karis's legacy was? Surely Edric

77

would have gone through the Will with her before the funeral, if she hadn't already been aware of exactly what was in it before then, and Karis would have expected Oliver to at least have given Kate a broad outline of what he intended to do with his estate and discussed it with her before drawing up his Will.

Karis mulled things over in her mind, wondering what to do. Of course she would write to Edric acknowledging his letter but perhaps she should ring him first just to have a chat about things generally. She might then be able to assess exactly how well, or otherwise, her legacy had gone down with Oliver's family.

"You didn't say anything," Jon said, looking at her accusingly. "You might have told me. Just think, Karis, you won't have to go out to work now will you? You'll be able to stay at home with me." Obviously the idea appealed to him as he smiled happily at her.

"Wait a minute, Jonathan. Don't let's get carried away here." Karis thought she should put the handbrake on before he got to mentally spend the money before they had even got it. "I know it sounds like a lot of money but we've literally got nothing in the bank at the moment. Nothing! I know we don't owe anybody any money but, all the same, it will be nice to have something to give us a bit of a cushion and to fall back on, and as regards the job, I'll think about that but my first instinct is to go for the interview anyway. I really don't feel old enough to want to be at home all day and every day just yet. Time enough for that in a few years time." She paused, and then added, "Perhaps we could have a holiday in the summer though. That would be good for both of us and give us something to look forward to." A fleeting image of them relaxing by the side of a pool in the sun, sipping long, cool drinks, passed through her head. Yes, she thought, they could both do with a break after such a bleak time recently.

"Always practical and sensible," Jon said, his tone of voice suggesting that he didn't want to be either and neither did he want Karis to be quite so straight-laced.

Some things never change, Karis sighed. She had always been the one to ensure that they didn't overspend on unnecessary things which they could do without while Jon was inclined to day-dream and expect everything to work out the way he thought it should regardless.

"Yes, you're right, Jon. I am going to be very sensible, at least until I find out a bit more. But being sensible doesn't stop me from feeling absolutely euphoric and very excited inside. I can't tell you exactly how I feel but it's like all my birthdays have come on one day, but given the choice, I would still rather have Oliver here than not." She stopped, blew her nose and said, "I'll just give Edric Longmore a call now and have a chat about things."

"Mrs Fielden. How nice of you to ring. You've got my letter then?" His voice was friendly.

"Yes, thank you. I must admit I am almost completely bowled over. I had no idea when you said that Oliver had left me a legacy that it would be so much. I really don't know what to say except thank you for letting me know, and please call me Karis."

Edric laughed. "You don't need to say anything, but I do hope that it is a nice surprise. I shall need your bank details so we can transfer the money to you as soon as possible. There are no strings attached, just a straight-forward gift of cash." He had liked Karis when he had met her and hoped that the unexpected windfall would benefit her as well as giving her a great deal of pleasure.

Karis wanted to ask about any other legacies or if Kate and her daughters were well cared for but she didn't quite know how to broach the subject. Almost as if reading her mind, Edric, without divulging client confidentiality, indicated that Kate would be staying at the house she had shared with Oliver and that her comfort and future had been well taken care of. He rightly assumed that anything he spoke to Karis about would remain confidential, having already mentioned to Karis that Oliver had been a wealthy man and that one hundred thousand pounds as part of his estate was really not a great deal of money in the general scheme of things.

"So if you can let me have those details, Karis, I'll get the transfer underway. Goodbye, and thank you for calling."

Karis put down the phone and sat staring into space. She needed time to think and there was a lot to think about. At present she and Jonathan shared a joint current account and a savings account which was just ticking over with a few hundred pounds which was lying dormant being too little to earn any appreciable interest; this was the residue from the sale of their house and the purchase of the cottage and was the total sum of their wealth, which was the reason that Karis had been so keen to get back to work.

But she couldn't help smiling; what an amazing piece of good fortune coming out of the blue. Thank you Oliver, she thought again. I am very grateful to you.

"What did he say?" Jonathan was hovering by her chair. "Do you get the money straight away? Perhaps we can go to Madeira this summer. We've always wanted to go there haven't we?" He was clearly excited like a child at the thought of having some money to spend again, his face animated and his blue eyes shining.

"Hang on a minute. Don't go so fast." She could see the money disappearing even before they had it. Perhaps she ought to put the money into a special account or an ISA maybe where it could earn some interest and where Jon couldn't get his hands on it. It wasn't that she considered the money hers alone, but on the other hand, she didn't want it disappearing quickly either. It would be nice just to savour the thought that they were no longer almost completely destitute. God knows the last few years had been a terrible worry and she didn't want to go through all that ever again so, anything that she could do to prevent that happening again would be done.

"I think I should go to the bank and have a chat with their financial advisers. What do you think?"

Jon shrugged his shoulders as though unconcerned or bothered about what she did. "Do what you like. After all, it is your money," and he turned away and went out into the garden.

Oh dear! That wasn't what she wanted at all but, on the other hand, she was determined that she wouldn't relinquish control over the money as she had before. Look where that had got them.

And the more she thought about the job, the more she thought that she would go ahead with the interview anyway. The legacy was great but it wasn't going to keep them in luxury and it was necessary that they had a regular income coming in between now and the time that they would start drawing their pensions. There was still a chance that she wouldn't get the job anyway, although she admitted to herself that she would be disappointed if she didn't. It sounded exactly the sort of thing that she felt she could do.

"Are you going to tell Jamie and Joanne?" Jonathan had come back in from the garden.

"I haven't got around to even thinking about that yet." Karis looked out of the window and noticed that there was a nuthatch on the nuts that they had hung up to encourage the birds into the garden. "Maybe I'll leave it for a few days and wait until it's all settled before I mention it. Did you see the nuthatch?"

Jonathan looked out of the window. "That's nice – we don't often see them. What's for lunch?" he smiled at her, his recent slight ill-temper seemingly put behind him.

The following day, Karis rang the bank and made an appointment to see the manager having said to Jon that she thought she ought to see him on her own and tell him about the legacy. Jonathan agreed, although somewhat reluctantly.

Mr Gordon, the bank manager, greeted her like an old friend, which, she mused, was probably due to his old fashioned style training and not due to the amount of money the bank was making out of their accounts. He had helped and advised them when Jon had lost his investment so was fully cognisant of their financial affairs, plus the recent sale and purchase of houses. "How nice to see you Mrs Fielden," he said, "How can I help you?"

"I'd like your advice please, Mr Gordon. I've been left a legacy of one hundred thousand pounds by an old friend who I worked for for several years and I am looking for the best possible means of investing it, or nearly all of it. I would like to put five thousand into the current account so that Jonathan and I may have a holiday in the summer and to give us a cushion for any unexpected or necessary spending and five thousand pounds for each of my children and then to invest the

82

rest." She smiled at him, "I consider myself very fortunate and a very lucky girl."

"You certainly are. That's wonderful news." He was, of course, used to handling large estates and very large legacies that had been left to people but he was genuinely pleased for Karis as he was personally familiar with her run of bad luck. "I've had a look at your accounts and am pleased to hear of your windfall as your income is so small and your outgoings exceed it and I was beginning to wonder what your plans were to improve the position.

He smiled at her. "How is your husband, Mrs Fielden? Is he back to full health again now?" He had been aware of Jon's ill health which had resulted from their run of very bad luck.

"He's much, much better thank you, although not quite perhaps ready for work just yet. He is still on medication but I don't think it will be too long before he is ready to put his nose to the grindstone again. Of course the type of illness he is suffering from is not as clear cut as some and it is difficult to define the line between fit and unfit. But, I am hopeful that he will soon be fully fit again." Living so closely with someone meant that often you failed to notice the small differences between being 'fine' and 'not being fine' although she felt that, mostly, Jonathan had overcome and got on top of his depression.

"I have an interview for a job next Wednesday which I am hopeful of securing, so with a little luck – another bit of luck – there should be a regular income to help out very soon with our everyday expenses." I'm definitely going to go for it, Karis thought, regardless of Jonathan's opinion.

"I wish you good luck with that then. Now, I think what I would advise is as follows..." And he then proceeded to tell her how he thought she should invest the money. "I'll put all the details in writing and give you a new account number and then you can spend some time going over it all before you make up your mind whether it is what you want to do. Then just give me a ring, either way, and I'll get it organised for you. Meantime, good luck with your job interview. I'm sure they will be very happy to have you working for them." He stood up and held out his hand. "It has been a pleasure to see you again, Mrs Fielden, thank you for coming to see me and I'm delighted that you've had such good news."

Karis felt that the meeting had gone very well but pondered on the way home how Jonathan would like what Mr Gordon was suggesting. Perhaps she should involve him more in the decisions that were likely to be made but she was extremely anxious to put most of the money away and out of reach so that it would give them a safety net for the future and, if she was honest, she was frightened and just didn't think she could trust Jonathan to do the right thing after what had happened previously.

Chapter 10

The letter duly arrived from the bank and Karis telephoned Edric Longmore with the details he needed to know. She had told Jonathan what Mr Gordon had suggested they should do with the money and after he had mulled it over in his mind for a while, he agreed with her that it all seemed very sensible, although he had reservations and it was obvious that it didn't meet with his wholehearted support. He often appeared to be lost in thought and far away but mostly he was cheerful and good-natured and Karis did her best to keep him that way by being upbeat herself.

Karis didn't really know and couldn't tell just how much the traumas of his illness after losing their nest-egg had damaged their relationship, but she felt that if she could keep things on a fairly even keel there was a chance that normality would eventually be resumed and Jonathan could then start to take on more of the responsibility for the daily running of their lives again. He was looking much fitter again and she, too, was feeling better herself because of the improvement in his health; the bonus of the legacy just gave them an extra boost and the closeness they had always felt was more in evidence again as they did the daily crossword together, went walking in the forest and enjoyed just being together.

Karis set off for her interview in a subdued mood, having become used to being at home and finding it difficult to get in the right frame of mind for work but she was determined to do as well as she could to make a good impression, secure new employment and get back into the working world once again as soon as possible.

She found the hospital with no trouble at all. It was down a long drive, set back off a country road in private grounds with plenty of trees and lawns surrounding the two-storey red-bricked building, probably built in the Edwardian era and looking slightly run-down but solid – definitely not an architectural gem. She parked her car in the visitor's car park and went into reception which was, as expected, just inside the main entrance hall of the building.

A woman in her fifties, with greying hair and wearing a blue twinset and a bored expression, her glasses perched on the end of her nose, looked up as she entered, smiled at Karis and asked if she could help. "I've come for a job interview," Karis said, and looking at the letter in her hand, smiled and added, "with Doctor Matthews." Karis knew very well from past employment that it was always a good idea to make a good impression and get on the right side of reception staff as they could be both very helpful and very obstructive and she wanted to set the right tone.

"Oh, yes. That will be in room forty. Follow this corridor straight past the stairs and you will find room forty on your right hand side. Dr Matthews will be in there."

"Thank you," Karis, smiled again, and then after a short walk down the corridor found room forty exactly where she had been told it would be. So far, so good. At least she was where she should be.

She knocked on the door and was told by a disembodied voice to "Come in," which she did.

Dr Matthews was a pleasant surprise. He was probably around forty or so, with tousled brown curly hair, brown eyes and a very pleasant smile. He was wearing a light tan tweed jacket over a pale green shirt and a striped golden coloured tie with dark brown trousers. He stood up to greet her as she came into the room, standing, she guessed at about six feet, shaking her hand firmly and asking her to take a seat. His eyes were kind as he looked directly into hers and said that he was very pleased to see her, he had read her CV which was very impressive and that he very much hoped that she would be able to help them, smiling all the while as he spoke. Karis liked what she saw, and felt her spirits rise; maybe this wouldn't be too much of an ordeal after all and would work out well for her.

"As you may know, Mrs Fielden," he went on, "we run a very busy hospital and the work ethic is such that we are usually working flat out and for long hours. The job we need you to help us with has been vacant for a couple of weeks so there is a back-log of work already. I think I should be honest with you and tell you that the lady who was doing the job found it all too much, having been with us for only a year or so and I can completely understand that it was too much for her to do and then go home and look after her family. I can only promise you more of the same, I'm afraid, but I can say that we will be very grateful if you feel you can give us a trial and help us out."

Karis listened carefully while Dr Matthews told her he was a psychiatrist and outlined the duties of the job to her. She would be working for a small group of doctors who each, in their own way, thought that they were more important than the others but were, in fact, all of equal importance as they supported each other and depended on each other's support for their work to be processed and carried out efficiently. Karis wondered where Dr Matthews figured in all this – was he the boss? She would, he said, share an office with two other female clerical staff, Jill and Angela, but would, effectively be in charge of administration. They each had their own computers and the usual offices and tea and coffee making facilities, with their office being situated on the other side of the corridor. The pay, when he eventually got around to it, almost as an afterthought, was not brilliant but it was reasonable, although the salary was set and there was no option of working for more hours for more money. Any overtime she did would have to be free gratis and for nothing except his thanks. Dr Matthews paused, smiled, and asked her if she needed to think about it or could she start next week?

Karis laughed. He was a lovely character and she was sure she could get on with him very well. Did she need time to think it over? No. She didn't think so.

"I'd be delighted to accept the job, Dr Matthews. But you may have to be patient with me as I haven't been working for the past few years and I may well be a bit rusty to start with, although it is probably like riding a bike, you never really forget although you may be a little unsteady to start with getting the wheels going in the right direction. And I think I can start next week but I will just have to check that out when I get home. Can I ring you in an hour or so just to confirm?"

He smiled at her. "I shall be keeping my fingers crossed," he said. "Thank you for coming in and I do hope that this is the start of a successful job for you and the solving of our current problems for us."

Karis drove the five miles home through mostly country lanes, with her head buzzing; so much to think about. Obviously the job would mean quite a change in how it would affect her personally, not to mention the change it would also mean for Jonathan, but surely the right sort of change and one that was needed.

The early onset of summer had brought the trees into full leaf and the hedgerows and banks were now full of bluebells and red campion, white cow parsley and lush grass. The sky was blue and cloudless and the air warm and fresh with so much promise of the summer to come. She suddenly felt lucky to be alive and full of anticipation of better times ahead. But what would Jon think? She just couldn't get out of the habit of consulting him and considering his opinion about everything and she doubted that she ever would.

She needn't have worried. "I think you should take it. Ring them up now right away and accept. You might not get the opportunity for anything else half as good, or not anything that is so tailor made for you anyway. The hours are OK, it is not too far away and the salary, though not great, is acceptable for a part-time job." Jon smiled at her. "I'll put the kettle on and make some tea," which seemed to be his answer to everything.

They sat companionably in the kitchen, with the door open to the garden letting the fresh air in. It was not quite warm enough to sit outside yet but a few more days like this and they'd be able to get the garden furniture out of hibernation and make use of it on the – what they euphemistically called – the patio.

"I should follow your example and find myself something to do. I mean, I shall follow your example," Jon stared into the middle distance while he stirred his tea. "I've made an appointment to see Dr Gregg on Friday morning. Hopefully he will give me the 'thumbs up' and I can get down to some serious job hunting myself. God knows what I am going to do but there must be something out there just waiting for me."

Karis looked at her husband, trying to see just how serious he was about getting a job. It was difficult to tell. He was looking fairly relaxed, not stressed-out and anxious but she knew only too well how quickly that could change. It only needed a small upset to make him lose his confidence and self-discipline and fall into doubt again about his ability to cope with everyday life.

"You'll find something, I'm sure, darling," she said reaching out her hand and caressing his cheek, wanting to reassure him. "Fate is just waiting round the corner to give you a helping hand. Just part-time would be ideal for you to make a start and then go on from there. Anyway, Dr Gregg will either give you the go-ahead or not, so we'd better wait until you've seen him before you start serious job hunting. But it is a step in the right direction."

Chapter 11

Karis looked out of the window as the plane banked slightly. She could see the runway to their right built, it appeared, on stilts over the sea and looking impossibly difficult for any passing pilot to land on easily! Madeira. She was so looking forward to spending a week there with Jon, doing nothing very much except explore the island, read a few books and eat some delicious food and generally re-charge her batteries. Wonderful!

She had agreed to spend a holiday there as Jonathan had been so keen on the idea, it being a place he had always wanted to visit. In a way it was to please him but now that they were almost there, she was determined that they should have as good a time as they possibly could, otherwise it would be a complete waste of time and money.

Dr Clegg, according to Jonathan, had been very pleased with the progress that Jon had made and had given him the all clear to start looking for a part-time job, which he had promised her he would do as soon as they got back home after the holiday. Since then, he had worked in the garden, had done some of the shopping and cooking while Karis had been at work and she thought that it was likely that the increase in the extra exercise he had been taking each day had helped in his recovery, giving him a definite feel-good factor.

In spite of her apprehension, their plane landed smoothly and without any obvious signs of difficulties; not really a surprise. They disembarked and were in the arrivals hall in no time at all, waiting impatiently for their luggage to arrive on the carousel and, once it was collected, went quickly outside the airport to look for the courtesy mini coach from the hotel where they were staying.

The sky was a brilliant blue. There were a few puffy white clouds sitting over the middle of the island where the highest hills were and the air was caressingly warm, although not too hot. They easily found the hotel coach with four other people in it who were fellow guests at the same hotel and after exchanging a few pleasantries, they were on their way.

The road into Funchal was recently built and, consequently, fast. Their hotel was on the western side of the town but the journey didn't take long and there was plenty to look at while they were travelling. Madeira is known as the Flower Island and it was easy to see why, thought Karis, having such a vast variety of flowers and colours everywhere. It was beautiful.

The hotel had been built within the last ten years and was, therefore, very modern. It had five floors built round an atrium which was full of real trees and plants and flowers and their room on the third floor had a balcony overlooking the sea. It was nicely furnished, had a super modern bathroom and shower and would do very nicely.

After unpacking their cases, they decided to explore the hotel's public rooms and grounds, stopping in the middle of their explorations for a drink and a bite to eat at the poolside bar. Several people were either swimming or lying on very comfortable looking loungers in the sun but Karis said she felt too lazy to get into her swimsuit so they just sat and relaxed.

It didn't take them long to find their way around the hotel which appeared to be fairly full with holidaymakers, mostly Brits but with a few Germans and some Japanese also staying there. There were two restaurants and entertainment each evening in the main restaurant, sometimes just a piano player but local dancers and musicians were also scheduled two evenings a week. And then there was dancing after dinner every evening to a trio of musicians if they felt like it.

On the first morning after their arrival they decided that they would plan for the next few days ahead and then just relax for the last two days. There was a local travel agent in the foyer who proved very helpful in helping them plan and book to see the best parts and special places of interest on the island and they were also insistent that they should have tea at Reid's Hotel one afternoon and also visit Blandy's, the Madeira wine company for some essential sampling of the local wine on another day. Having arranged for all that, the two of them were content to take a taxi into Funchal so that they could explore the town and have some lunch out while they did so.

They both loved the island. Everywhere you looked there were flowers; agapanthus flowering at the side of all the roads and roses, fuchsias and every other flower and shrub you could think of, tumbling over walls and flourishing in gardens so that there was a riot of colour everywhere you looked. "I wish I could paint," Karis said. "This island must be an artist's paradise. No wonder Churchill loved coming here."

And the market, full of noisy, busy people, was well worth a visit too. Not only for the abundance of flowers in every possible shade and shape creating a riot of colour but also to see the variety of fruit for sale and the choice of fish too, some they had never heard of before. "It almost makes me want to buy something to take back and cook," Karis remarked. "Almost!"

Jon laughed, "Me, too. Imagine having somewhere like this on our doorstop to shop from. There wouldn't be a problem choosing something different to eat every night would there?"

They had lunch at a little bistro with a garden, sitting outside under the shade of a tree, sharing a bottle of wine, relaxed and more than content with their choice of holiday.

Idly, Karis's thoughts, out of nowhere, turned to their honeymoon in Tanzania in 1975. That, too, was a very colourful country so maybe that was what had made her think about it. Her mother and father had paid for everything for them as a wedding present as, still very young and not having, as yet, made much headway in their jobs, they couldn't at the time they married, afford to pay for much more than a weekend in a B & B! Apart from giving them a taste for the exotic and extravagant, it also gave them a thirst for travel and a desire to explore the world which, apart from a few beach holidays in Europe, hadn't so far been fulfilled, mainly because Jamie and then Joanne had arrived earlier than originally planned and radically changed their lives.

Karis smiled to herself. How young they had been; almost totally innocent and unprepared for the experience of mixing with the sophisticated travellers and decadent ex-pats they met when they stayed at Lake Manyara; we were no more than just a couple of kids really.

The hotel at Lake Manyara was built on an escarpment overlooking the lake, with wooded hillsides below it and to the right; to the left the terrain was flat and mostly consisted of grazing plains which disappeared into a hazy blue horizon. The hotel consisted of a long, low one storey white building with the brilliant orange Golden Showers honeysuckle-type flowers tumbling in a riot of colour, over the roof and down some of the walls to the ground. The colourful gardens were filled with frangipani, bougainvillea, blue and white agapanthus, cannas, and yesterday, today and tomorrow all growing in island beds which were randomly set in green lawns which needed almost constant watering and were the pride and joy of the many "shambas" – gardeners - employed by the hotel.

Most of the guest bedrooms and suites faced the lake and had individual patios where you could sit and drink sun-downers while taking in the beauty of the lake. Karis and Jon were surprised to find on their first evening there that there was only a very short time between the sun going down and total darkness, a period of about half an hour when the air turned pink and was, usually, very still. The large figure-eight swimming-pool was built slightly to the right as you looked down at the lake and was surrounded by a mosaic of blue and white tiles and the carefully nurtured lawn.

During the day, it was not unusual to see elephants walking slowly in groups by the lake and also, if you were lucky, lions – sometimes, sprawled in the lower branches of the trees and giraffes, gnu or buffalo in the distance; most guests had binoculars at the ready for just such a treat.   The hotel was literally miles from anywhere but was kept serviced by a fleet of small aircraft that landed on an airstrip built for the convenience of guests and the delivery of supplies, a mile or so to the rear of the hotel. The only other means of getting to the hotel was by way of a murram road which was either extremely dusty or, in the rainy seasons, turned into thick mud and was difficult to drive on in an ordinary car, which was why most people used ancient 4 x 4s.

Karis smiled to herself as she remembered one particularly warm evening when, after a more than somewhat protracted dinner of prawns, guinea fowl, cheese and then mango sorbet, which had been complemented by a bottle of very acceptable wine, they had fallen into conversation with another young couple who were on a long weekend visit from Nairobi where they lived and worked. He, Laurie, had flown them down in an aircraft hired for the weekend which, Karis and Jonathan surmised, they did on a fairly regular basis. Laurie, they soon found out, had been born in Kenya to parents who had also been born in the country and Cara, his wife, who Karis wanted to dislike because she was so gorgeous with long beautiful red-gold hair and a figure to die for, had also been born in Nairobi. Between them, they appeared to have it all – good looks and jobs, a lovely home, plenty of money and a zest for life that was catching.

Laurie ordered a bottle of champagne and invited Karis and Jon to join them at their table on the terrace outside the restaurant. Already feeling the effects of half a bottle of wine and a pre-dinner gin and tonic, Karis wasn't at all sure that they should but Jonathan accepted immediately and said they'd be delighted to. It was the start of a memorable night.

Aided by the wine, which no doubt assisted the easy flow of conversation between them, coupled with plenty of laughter as they discovered many things in common, Laurie and Jonathan were soon the best of friends. Karis and Cara were a little slower in their mutual liking of each other but soon found that they, too, had a lot in common. To start with, they were much the same age and though they lived in separate, and very different countries, fashion was international and they both loved pretty clothes and shoes. Nairobi, Cara said, had a good quota of select boutiques and shoe shops and it was a pity that Karis was not stopping there on their way back to the UK as she would love to show her around.

The champagne disappeared fairly quickly and Laurie ordered another bottle. Karis made a half-hearted protest saying that she was far too tipsy already but Jonathan and Cara agreed that another bottle would be good. They were not alone as several guests at other tables were also enjoying the evening and getting very noisy, blocking out the sound of the cicadas and the noises of the African night which was now very dark but with a sky that was full of a million bright stars.

It was a magic place and Karis gave herself up to the sheer pleasure of being alive, especially when Jonathan leaned over to her, caressing her back and shoulders as he did so; a simple gesture with a lot of promise. And then Laurie had suggested a swim. Karis looked at him trying to make up her mind whether he really meant it or not but he obviously did. "I'll have to go and get my swimming things," she said and laughed when he said she didn't need to do that as they could skinny dip! Was he serious? She looked at Jonathan whose face was creased in a permanent smile, obviously under the influence of too much alcohol and everyone's friend; there was no way he was going to disagree. And Cara was obviously ready to join in as she was already starting to walk towards the pool, discarding her shoes as she went. What to do?

It was a 'when in Rome' situation! Karis followed Cara who, by this time had pulled her dress over her head and was standing by the pool in her bra and pants. There was not much light from the hotel which was about fifty yards away but enough to see Cara's body looking slim and lovely, and in another few seconds, there was a splash and Cara was in the pool saying that the water was lovely and to come on in. Aware that Jon and Laurie were just behind her, Karis pulled her clothes off and jumped into the water, catching her breath as she did so but loving the sensuous feeling of the water swirling round her body. It was delicious, cool and caressing. Why didn't they always swim that way?

Karis was suddenly aware of someone close behind her as she trod water and then felt hands caressing her breasts. She automatically turned round , thinking it was Jonathan, only to find in the semi-darkness that she was clutching at Laurie. "Sorry! I thought you were Jon."

He grinned at her, his teeth gleaming in the dusky light. "Don't apologise, darling. It's good to have a change now and again, don't you think? You have beautiful tits." Karis had been horrified, swimming away from him as quickly as she could, embarrassed and glad that no one could really see her face as she was sure she was scarlet. But neither Jon or Cara had noticed and were chatting and laughing together while floating on their backs in the black water.

The four of them swam around a bit, laughing and chatting to each other for about twenty minutes and then Karis suddenly felt tired and cold and wanted to go to bed. "Jon. I've had enough now. I think I'll get out. Are you coming?" Karis was wondering how she was going to make a dignified naked exit from the pool. I guess there is nothing for it, she thought, just climb out as if I was wearing my swimsuit, grab my clothes and throw my dress over my head and walk back into the hotel. What else could she do?

"I'm coming too. Wait for me Karis. Good idea of yours though, Laurie. We must do it again sometime, but meantime, my wife needs an escort so I'd better go. Goodnight, both. Lovely meeting you and we've had a ball." Jonathan climbed up the pool steps, his wet body shining in the dim light. Together, holding hands and clutching their underclothes in their other hands, they made their way back to their room, Jon wearing just his

98

shirt and Karis her wet dress, feeling both sheepish and exhilarated at the same time.

Most guests had gone to bed by this time as many were scheduled for very early safari trips in the morning so, getting to their room was not a problem and they saw no-one except staff who, well used to all manner of unusual behaviour from their guests, turned a blind eye and pretended not to notice.

Karis towelled her hair dry and pulling the mosquito net aside, climbed into bed, relaxed, slightly tipsy and very happy. Jonathan quickly joined her, pulling her to him and kissing her thoroughly on the mouth. "Well that was a different way to spend an evening, wasn't it?" he laughed. "What happened to all your inhibitions?"

"What happened to yours?" she asked.

Up until this night and because at first they had been so tired after all the celebrations of their wedding and then the long journey out to East Africa, their lovemaking had been tentative and exploratory. They were still discovering each other's bodies, hampered to a large extent by their shyness but suddenly that was all behind them. For the first time, unshackled by either shyness or inhibition, they made love that came close to being perfect. Karis, suffused with love for her husband, thought she would never experience such a feeling ever again.

The days passed quickly and they had been in Madeira for four days when Karis noticed that Jonathan was often looking pensive, as if his thoughts were far away. She wondered if she should mention it but decided against it as she thought that he was probably just mulling through thoughts about going back to work and he wasn't a natural chatterer anyway. However, after another day passed and he appeared to be withdrawing into himself even more, she became anxious and decided that she would have to say something.

"Is anything the matter, darling? You're not feeling ill are you, only you've been awfully quiet for the last couple of days? Do you want to talk about it?" She smiled at him trying to lighten his mood.

"No. Nothing. I was just thinking about going back to work."

"Oh, I see. I thought it might be something like that." She smiled, relieved. "Well at least we've had a nice break and the weather has been perfect, so we shall have something to look back on when we're busy at our jobs." In fact, Jon was looking very handsome as he had developed a tan and in spite of his withdrawn look, she thought how much she fancied him.

They were getting dressed for dinner, neither of them in a hurry as they were not particularly hungry having eaten well at lunchtime when Karis put her arms round him, stood on her tiptoes and kissed him on the mouth. "We could always go down later on," she said, thinking of their honeymoon and looking up at him hoping that he would think of it too and kiss her back. But she was disappointed. Jonathan pushed her away.

"No. I think we should go down at our usual time," he said, turning away picking up his jacket and shrugging into it.

"OK." She wasn't going to argue. And she wasn't going to feel rebuffed either.

Dinner that night was an almost silent meal, only the obligatory polite words being spoken between them. Karis tried to make conversation but Jon didn't respond so after a while she thought it would be better if she just kept quiet. She was filled with foreboding wondering just what was wrong.

The next day dawned, as usual, sunny and warm. Karis turned over in bed and looked over to Jon's bed to see if he was awake but the bed was empty. Momentarily panic-stricken, she threw the bedclothes off and jumped out of bed and just at that moment he came in from the balcony. "Darling, there you are! I thought for a moment I had lost you. Are you all right? Couldn't you sleep?" She was still struggling to be fully awake having slept very deeply herself but not being able to see Jonathan had given her a nasty shock. Stop being so stupid, she told herself. Of course he is all right.

"I didn't sleep very well and have been awake for ages. I've just been on the balcony thinking over a few things." His tone was quiet and measured but he looked unhappy and Karis's feeling of foreboding, that she had last evening, returned.

"I'm sorry, darling. Perhaps you should tell me what is worrying you." She picked up her dressing gown and put it on, brushed her hair quickly and then sat down looking at him. "I'm all ears," she said and laughed nervously.

Jonathan stood looking at her, thinking how lovely she looked and then he sat down opposite her and put his head in his hands. Karis felt her heart thump and her pulse begin to quicken but she said nothing, just waited for him to speak.

It took him a minute or two and then he said, "I've been thinking about all that money that Oliver left you. It seems to me that it was an awful lot just for working for him. Did you have an affair with him?"

Karis stared at him, recalling, suddenly, how he had mentioned at the time she received the letter telling her of the legacy that he thought it had been a big thank-you in return for typing a few letters. He had obviously become obsessed with the thought and as is often the case when a thought takes hold, it grows and takes on a new dimension and in his case he had managed to turn a maybe into a definite. Dear God, what to say?

Before she could think what to say to him, he said, "It seems to me that I have been enjoying this holiday on another man's money and the more I thought about it, the more obvious it became. Why would Oliver give you so much unless there was more to his relationship with you than you said," his voice becoming raised as his thoughts came tumbling out of his mouth.

Karis stood up and glared at Jonathan, too angry to speak at first. "I'm not even going to dignify your accusation with a reply," she said and went into the bathroom, slamming the door behind her. What had got into him? The holiday had started so well and they were, she thought, having a wonderful time exploring the island, swimming, and having romantic dinners in the evenings, and even their somewhat spasmodic love life had perked up to, she thought, their mutual enjoyment.

Hang on a minute, she told herself, you don't want him to have another nervous breakdown, you've got to handle this carefully so that he doesn't go into a depression again. How ironic, she thought, she had believed that the money would be such a help in getting them really back on their feet again and all it appeared to be doing was driving them apart. Dear Oliver, she thought, what have you done?

The strength of the power shower and the heat of the water calmed her nerves as she tried to think how best to handle the situation. She would have to put her own feelings of dismay behind her and let Jonathan know that he came first with her, that what he felt mattered more than anything else; he needed reassurance, so she would try and give it to him.

She quickly towelled herself dry, threw her dressing-gown back on and went back into the bedroom. Jon was sitting out on the balcony again, staring into space. "Sorry, darling. We've obviously got some talking to do. Do you want to go first and try and tell me exactly what you've been thinking these last few days?"

Jonathan looked at her and made an attempt at a smile. "I didn't mean to go on about it, it's just that one thought led to another and then I was on a roller-coaster and I just couldn't stop." He looked apologetic. "I'll try and put it out of my mind and I'm sorry if I've upset you. Obviously I trust you and I don't really think you've been unfaithful, it's just that I had this thought and it got out of control."

Karis did her best to smile back at him but it was a very half-hearted attempt. She was hurt and puzzled by his train of thought. "Ok. Let's try and forget about it and go and have some breakfast. I think we should make the best of the couple of days we have left before we go home..." her voice trailed away as she realised that he was probably still going to be thinking that he was on holiday making use of another man's money.

They spent the morning lazing by the pool, occasionally going for a swim and then lunching on locally caught fish with a bottle of well-chilled wine at the pool bar. It was all idyllic but in spite of their best efforts, the magic had gone. Neither of them wanted to talk and both pretended to read books, going over and over again the same page which made no more sense at the third time of reading than it did the first. Karis just wished that the time would pass as quickly as possible and that they could get on the plane home. Jonathan was quiet but he didn't appear to be unhappy, although Karis felt sure that underneath his calm manner there was still a lot of unease just beneath the surface.

It was a relief to both of them to board the plane for the flight home. Any one observing their demeanour would have had no conception at all of the unhappiness that they were both feeling. Perhaps getting back to their home and a 'normal' routine would restore an even keel; Karis could only hope so. This present uncomfortable feeling between them, almost as if they were strangers, was driving her to despair: she'd been there, she'd done that and she didn't want to go through all that again.

Chapter 12

Within six weeks of their holiday, Jonathan found a job. It was only part-time, working four days a week in the accounts department of a local small factory which sold packaging materials and made cardboard boxes. The pay was relatively low but the office was within walking distance of the bus which he could use for the time being and which he could get on and be at work within thirty minutes or so. He seemed very pleased but not unnaturally felt a bit apprehensive as he hadn't worked for some time and, consequently, felt out of touch with the working world. However, Karis was determined that she would give him as much support as she could to boost his confidence, telling him that he could do the job with his eyes closed, which she really thought he could.

With their combined salaries they would be able to pay the bills for the house and live reasonably well without having to touch the legacy which they could draw on for holidays or special treats and, of course, they also had a son and a daughter who would both probably decide to get married one day so it would come in handy for that when the time came.

No mention had been made by either of them of their holiday row once they got home. Karis went back to work and Jonathan resumed looking after the house and garden, all the time promising to try and get a job so, when he did, she was delighted. He appeared to be relaxed and untroubled and was affectionate and caring with Karis to such an extent that she wondered sometimes whether she had dreamt the whole ghastly episode.

It was difficult for Karis to concentrate on her own work on the day that Jonathan started back at work as she found her thoughts constantly wondering how he was getting on, at the same time doing her own job which had become more demanding since she first started it. She was given more and more to do as Dr Matthews and his colleagues couldn't believe their luck in finding someone to help them who didn't constantly grumble about the increase in workload. She did suggest to him that perhaps she could work for four days instead of three but he said that their budget wouldn't run to that and adding how very grateful they were to her for her efforts in helping to keep them up to date and in order.

"You should market that," she said to him one day.

"What's that?" he asked.

"Soft soap. You'd make a fortune," she replied with a smile. She had become good friends with Dr Matthews and she did wonder, once or twice, whether she should mention Jonathan's depression since it was within his area of expertise and she would be happy to receive any help in trying to understand Jonathan's problems, but had decided against it as it wasn't ethical to talk about personal problems and Jon, at present at least, seemed to be doing OK and he didn't appear, at least on the surface, to have any problems, either major or minor, during the days before he started his new job.

Karis arrived home about ten minutes before Jonathan came in the door, whistling softly to himself. She kissed him on the mouth, looking anxiously into his eyes to try and read how the day had gone. He kissed her back lightly, drew back and smiled briefly before disentangling himself from her arms and taking off his jacket.

"How was it? Did it go OK? Have you got some nice people in the office that you like and can get on with?" Karis realised that she was babbling. "Sorry, but I've been thinking of you all day. I'll get you a cup of tea, or would you like something stronger?"

Jonathan sat down heavily on one of the kitchen chairs, put his hand up and smoothed his hair, sighing as he did so. "I feel exhausted, although I haven't done much in the way of work, just meeting my fellow workers, finding out what is expected from me, reading about the company, trying to memorise our customers...there are a lot of them. A cup of tea would be lovely." He then sat quietly, lost in thought.

Jon sipped his tea. "That's nice, better than the rubbish that comes out of the vending machine anyway, but it is free and free is good, I guess."

"You might go in tomorrow then?" Karis said, trying to make him smile but wondering as she said it whether he might think she was giving him the option.

He looked at her, trying to make his mind up whether she was serious and decided that she was only joking. "I might. I'll give it some thought. What's for dinner?"

"I've retrieved a beef stroganoff from the freezer. I thought we'd have that with some rice and some sugar snap peas with spiced plums and crème fraiche and cheese and biscuits. Will that do, do you think? Are you hungry?"

"It all sounds more than OK and yes, I am hungry. I think I'll just go and change and get into something more comfortable now. Do you need a hand with anything?" His tone of voice was gentle and measured which Karis found reassuring, as she had been so anxious about whether he would be able to cope with the stresses and strains of work again.

"No thanks. There's not much to do. Dinner will be ready in half an hour then."

It was after Jonathan had been at work a couple of weeks and their lives had settled into a routine again which they both were comfortable with that Karis received a letter from Kate Melrose. It was brief, merely stating that, if possible, she would very much like to see Karis either at The Pheasants, Kate's home, or perhaps they could meet for lunch somewhere in Winchester. Would Karis please ring her. Karis turned the letter over in her hand expecting perhaps to see an explanation why Kate would want to see her but, of course, the reverse page was blank.

Karis was puzzled. "I've no idea why she wants to see me," she said to Jonathan. "We've never been particularly friendly. Maybe she is feeling a bit lonely and would like some company but I'm sure she has lots of friends so I don't really think that that is the reason. And I'm sure the girls visit fairly regularly, so why me?"

Jonathan was non-committal, muttering that she didn't have to go if she didn't want to. "No, I know that. Perhaps she needs some help with some administration. She didn't have to do anything while Oliver was alive, he, or I, did it all. I think that that is the most likely explanation."

Having decided that that was what it must be about, she put the letter to one side and got on with what she was doing, deciding that she would ring Kate the following day as there was no great need to rush to get in touch.

"Thank you for calling Karis," Kate said, her voice warm and friendly, "would you like to come here for lunch next Thursday? Around 12ish? Good. I'll look forward to seeing you then." The phone call had been brief and gave nothing away regarding why Kate wanted to see her.

"I shall look forward to seeing you then."

Karis was puzzled but she shrugged her shoulders; she would find out soon enough what it was all about.

It took Karis about forty minutes to drive to The Pheasants the following Thursday, avoiding the main arterial route and driving through country roads that were flanked by lush and vigorous green growth, although the temperature itself was cooler than it had been recently. She had put on a light-weight blue trouser suit and, although a little anxious about what Kate might want to see her about, she thought how good it was to have a day out of her usual routine, away from work and the house - and Jonathan.

Since Jonathan had been back at work, Karis's anxiety for his health had gradually decreased as he gave every appearance of someone who was relaxed and able to do the job while enjoying his leisure time at home with Karis. Occasionally she would get a glimpse of his struggle to contain his irritation at what he perceived to be an injustice at work or something that made the news headlines that he didn't agree with, but that was minimal and overall, her awareness of the slightest change in his demeanour began to be less of a strain and she felt that maybe she, too, could relax a bit more, although she knew that it was possible that depression could easily rear its ugly head again with very little logical reason.

He never referred again to his outburst about her legacy or her supposed affair while they were on holiday, and he had either forgotten about it, which she doubted, or he had other things on his mind which were enough to keep him from thinking the unthinkable. He renewed his membership at the gym and made full use of the pool and equipment, spending at least four hours a week there and what with keeping the garden looking pristine and pretty, he didn't have a lot of spare time to indulge in speculating about what might have been.

Karis allowed her thoughts to roam around at random while she drove, enjoying the time to herself and before she knew it she was turning into the driveway to The Pheasants.

The Pheasants was beautiful and she caught her breath as she thought how wonderful it must be to own a property like that and not have to worry about where the next month's mortgage was coming from. The house was built of stone, honey colour mellowed with age; it had four gabled windows on the first floor and three large windows on the ground floor, an arched porch-way sheltering an oak door between the first and third windows. Pink and red climbing roses had been planted on either side of the porch and these were climbing up the walls of the house and were in full bloom, with a few fallen petals lying on the gravel. A large herbaceous border full of perennials in full colour was to the left of the house as you approached it, and this was in front of a six foot wall, which protected the house from the north winds. Fruit trees, peaches and pears, had been trained against the wall.

Karis got out of the car, picked up her handbag and walked towards the front door. Before she had time to ring the bell, the door was opened by Kate looking very pretty in a pale mauve silk dress, her almost white hair carefully styled in soft curls, a smile of welcome on her lips.

"Karis. How lovely to see you. Thank you for coming. Please come in." She extended her hand and they briefly shook hands as Karis stepped into the hallway. This was a square, good-sized room, with a staircase of dark oak spindles and rail going up the wall to the right leading to a galleried landing. A door, one of several leading off from the hall, to the left through which they walked, took them into the sitting room.

"The garden is looking beautiful, Kate. Obviously your gardener is kept busy keeping it all in such pristine order." Karis smiled, thinking of their own tiny little patch at home which required very little maintenance having been planted with climbers, mostly clematis and roses, against the wall and large wooden static tubs filled with flowering shrubs and bulbs standing in the pea gravel.

"Yes, it is, isn't it? Ben does a very good job for me. No prompting necessary. He just gets on with it. I think he was very well schooled by Oliver so he knows exactly what needs to be done and then does it. Marvellous! I don't even have to pay him as the bank transfers his wage into his bank account each month and that takes care of that. One less worry."

The sitting room was approximately twenty feet square with a large window to the front and a French window leading out onto the patio at the back of the house. It was furnished with two huge four-seater sofas and a couple of easy chairs all covered in cream coloured chintz with differing shades of apricot and peach flowers and green leaves, plus an assortment of side tables and bookcases in dark oak and two large rugs of brown, fawn and ochre colours on the dark oak parquet flooring, which was polished. The walls were the colour of clotted cream, which showed off the various paintings to their best advantage, including a lovely portrait of Kate taking pride of place on the wall over the huge fireplace which was also built of honeyed stone. Oliver had commissioned it for Kate's 50th birthday and it was a very good likeness; in it she was wearing a beautiful blue silk gown and was smiling faintly as if she found life amusing. A fire basket was laid with logs, and a large bowl of mixed summer flowers on one of the small tables completed the room.

"Please sit down, Karis. Would you like coffee or can I offer you a glass of nice cold wine?"

"What a beautiful room, Kate. I'd forgotten just how lovely it is." Karis had been to The Pheasants on a few occasions, usually work-related and not socially as Oliver liked to keep his business separate from his home life, so she hadn't had a chance to study the house before. "A cup of coffee would be very welcome, thank you."

Karis sat on one of the arm chairs, sinking into the cushions, while Kate left the room to get the coffee. She was back almost immediately, carrying a tray set with cups and saucers, a plate of biscuits, a coffee pot and a small jug of cream.

"I still have Jill working for me as my housekeeper," she said, by way of explanation for her early return. "She has agreed to stay as long as I want her to, which is a great blessing, as I couldn't possibly manage without her. She has retained her small cottage in the village and visits it frequently, staying there at weekends when I have the family staying here with me. But now she has no one else to think about, her children having grown up and left home, she is happy to sleep here during the week. It's a comfort to know that there is someone else in this big house."

She poured Karis a cup of coffee and offered her sugar and cream, both of which Karis accepted, declining the biscuits.

Karis waited for Kate to bring up the subject of why she was there. Obviously not just yet, as Kate was busy telling her all about her grandchildren and then went on

112

to say that she was kept busy with her bridge club, her WI meetings and also her art classes which she went to weekly in the next village. It sounded almost idyllic but Kate spoke quickly as though she wanted to convince Karis that everything in her world was all right and that she hadn't a moment to spare in which to feel sorry for herself.

Occasionally, when asked, Karis answered Kate with replies concerning her own life and also Jonathan and Jamie and Joanne but she still got the feeling that Kate was biding her time, although she did express an interest when Karis told her she was working at her local learning disabilities hospital and wanted to know how she liked it and what she thought of how the system worked.

Eventually, Kate said, "I expect you are ready for something to eat. Let's go into the dining room. Jill has prepared us some soup, a quiche and a salad – I hope that is all right for you?"

"That's sounds lovely and just the sort of food I like. Thank you."

As anticipated, the food was simple but delicious and Karis was enjoying it very much, the conversation although not exactly flowing easily between them, was natural enough as is usual between two mature women, when out of the blue, just as she was about to help herself to a second piece of quiche, Kate suddenly said, "Did you have an affair with Oliver?"

Karis stared at Kate, her arm in mid air with a slice of quiche on the server. Dear God, she thought to herself, not you as well! Quickly she recovered her poise and put the quiche back on its plate, her appetite suddenly completely gone.

"Is that why you asked me to come here Kate, so that you could ask me that?" Her voice was calm but the whole of her body was trembling. "I thought that perhaps you wanted me to help you with some administration or something like that. I certainly wouldn't have come if I'd had any inkling at all that you were going to ask me that."

Kate, too, appeared to be in some discomfort, her blue eyes shining with unshed tears. "I did Karis. I mean I do – want you to help with some cataloguing that Oliver was going to do but never got around to. All our photographs and his books and our music collection need to be put in some sort of order, there is so much to do and I just can't manage it..." her voice trailed away to silence and she wiped away her tears with a handkerchief.

And then she recovered her composure and said, "I'm so sorry Karis, it was just something Sara said that made me wonder and I've been wondering ever since and I couldn't sleep worrying about it so I thought the only way to resolve it was to ask you over for lunch and then, maybe, talk things through. It was wrong of me and I wish I hadn't said anything because I would still like you to help me out with the cataloguing and I feel that I've spoiled our friendship now."

It was hardly a friendship, Karis thought to herself, but having got over the initial shock she was back in control of her feelings and her reactions to Kate. However, they needed to get things settled between them. "What exactly did Sara say?" she asked.

"Just that it was a lot of money that Oliver had left you and she wondered why since you had only worked for him for seven or eight years or so. She didn't actually mention an affair. I just picked up that that was probably what she was thinking. She did say, though, that the money was more than he had left his grandchildren..." and again her voice trailed off and she glanced down at her plate. "Would you like anything else to eat Karis?" she said, her good manners overcoming her distress.

"No thank you Kate. I couldn't eat another thing. But I think that perhaps we should talk so that we can clear the air and you can then have some peace of mind and then be able to sleep at night."

Together they left the dining room and returned to the sitting room, Karis going back to the chair she had sat in before lunch. She thought about what she wanted to say.

"You knew Oliver better than anyone, Kate, so you know what sort of man he was, forthright, meticulous in his planning and expecting everyone to do their job to the best of their ability – which, for a man in his position, I don't think was unreasonable. He was fair in his treatment of his staff, but tough on those who thought that perhaps they could get away with doing a job that wasn't quite as good as it should be. He worked long hours, was constantly thinking of ways to improve the company and was, on a personal basis, kindness itself. Definitely his bark was much worse than his bite." She paused, wondering if she should go on and decided she hadn't finished yet.

"Obviously, I worked closely with Oliver; as his PA it was part of my job. I shielded him from unwanted attention, planned his days and made sure that he was where he should be at any given time. I took care of his travel arrangements, making sure everything was correct, in order and the way it should be and also, as you know, often helped with the holidays you took together. And all that, of course, was besides the correspondence, e-mails and appointments with all of his business associates and other companies. I worked very hard, often for long hours but I enjoyed my job and found it very rewarding. Why he left me the money he did I don't know, but I have to say that it was very unexpected and totally out of the blue, and I am very grateful to him as life has been more than a little tough over the past few years and he has afforded me a financial cushion for which I am very grateful. Always and at all times you and Jane and Sarah were his first consideration, particularly you, and he made no secret of that fact, ever." She stopped talking, suddenly overcome with sadness and regret that Oliver was no longer alive and thinking that she would miss him for as long as she lived. He had enriched her life in so many ways.

Kate sat quietly in her chair, her hands folded in her lap and tears slowly sliding down her cheeks. She wiped them away and said, "I'm so sorry, Karis. It's just that I miss him so much that at times it's just like a physical pain. I don't want pity, just understanding. Sometimes, there doesn't seem to be a reason for getting out of bed in the mornings. I rattle around this house like a lost soul wondering what to do with myself. I can't concentrate on a book, no TV programmes appeal and I don't even, really, want to play bridge or go to the WI. I enjoy my painting because I can lose myself in it but it is only a temporary respite and as soon as I stop I feel lost and alone again."

Karis was a little taken by surprise at Kate's outpouring of grief and wondered what she should say. "Does Sara still come and see you at weekends?" she asked. "And what about Jane and her family? Couldn't you perhaps go and stay with them now and again, do some shopping, see a show or exhibition or something? I'm sure they would love to have you and they would understand your loneliness and unhappiness. And it would also get you away from being here alone and missing Oliver so much."

Kate had dried her tears and was looking composed again. "Sara does come most weekends but she has her own life to lead and her business to run and I don't want her to feel that she is obliged to come and check up on me to make sure I am OK. And Jane has invited me to stay but I've put it off so far. Perhaps I should give it more thought. I need to get on with life, get used to being on my own and cope, but it is so very hard."

The day had taken on a completely different direction from that which Karis had expected. She was still mulling over in her head the thought that Kate had practically accused her of having an affair with Oliver and, at the same time, wanted her to help her with some neglected administration. Obviously, she was feeling very unhappy and lonely but if she really thought that Karis had had an affair with her husband why would she want Karis to be anywhere near her. It didn't make sense. But then bereavement, especially when it is totally unexpected, can cause people to act unpredictably and out of character and Kate appeared to be still in shock.

Feeling that she should try and do something to help Kate feel better, Karis said, "If you would still like me to come over one day a week or fortnight to help out with the cataloguing, I'd be happy to do so, Kate. I work three days a week – they can't afford to pay me for more than that on their budget – but I could spare one day, possibly Thursdays, if that would suit you."

"That sounds great Karis. I'd really like to get it all sorted out and tidy but there is quite a lot to do. And of course I would pay you. I wouldn't expect you to do it for nothing." Kate managed a smile as she spoke.

"Thank you Kate. Shall we leave it until I've put everything in order and then see. Obviously, at the moment, I have no idea how long it will take but I will keep a log of my hours, or maybe you would just like to pay me a lump sum. I am happy either way and I am sure we can work something out together. Now, I really must be going. Jonathan is home from work today and I don't want to be too late getting back." She rose from the chair, picked up her bag and held out her hand to Kate.

"Thank you for lunch, Kate. It was delicious. I'll ring you to confirm when I shall be starting work, but it will probably be the week after next, and I shall look forward to that. Now, I'll see myself out. Goodbye for now."

And with that she walked out of the room, out of the front door and drove away, her mind still in a state of confusion from what had been said since her arrival at The Pheasants.

Chapter 13

The drive home seemed to take less time than the drive to The Pheasants. Once she got on to the dual carriageway Karis put her foot down and drove as fast as the speed limit allowed. Her head was in a mess and her normal logical way of thinking about problems had deserted her. She wondered whether she should tell Jonathan what had happened; he was obviously going to want to hear all about Kate and why she had been invited to lunch. Well, that was OK, because there was a perfectly good reason why she had done so, there was absolutely no need, though, for her to tell him about Sarah's suspicions so she would keep that bit to herself; no point in adding fuel to the fire.

It was disturbing to think that Jonathan had voiced the same thoughts, particularly as Helen, when she had bumped into her in town, had also mentioned that Karis and Oliver had been 'so close'. Well, that was true enough, they had been but their relationship had always been very professional, albeit friendly. I'll just have to put it down to people putting two and two together and coming up with five, she thought

What will Jonathan think about me going over to The Pheasants to work? It was possible that he wouldn't like it at all but having agreed with Kate that she would help out, she couldn't now renege on her promise, but then the job shouldn't take long anyway; a few weeks should see it finished. And she could always leave home in the morning after he left for work and be home again before he returned so it shouldn't really be a problem. He was still working four days a week but hints had been dropped that his hours were likely to be increased soon if he was willing to take on more work and he had indicated that he was.

She was busy in the kitchen preparing the food for dinner when she heard Jon's key in the lock. He came into the kitchen looking tired and drawn, pecked her on the cheek, picked up *The Times* and sat down heavily at the kitchen table. "I've had a rotten day, what has yours been like?" he said, already turning the pages of the paper over and passing comment on the editorial which didn't please him. Clearly, something had upset him at work and he wasn't, just then, interested in her day at all so it was likely that anything she said to him would either be of no interest or would be misconstrued so she decided that she would just leave it for a while and wait for him to calm down a bit.

"Why don't you have a nice relaxing bath, Jon? Dinner will be ready in about an hour so you have plenty of time to unwind and try and forget the hard part of the day – perhaps after all it wasn't as bad as you thought."

"Mmm. I think that's a very good idea," he said and disappeared up the stairs. Shortly after the water finished filling the bath, Karis heard Jonathan's light baritone voice murdering a popular song – he was obviously beginning to wind down; she was hopeful that the evening would prove to be less stressful than it had looked like it was going to be.

In fact, their evening was quiet, neither of them being in a talkative mood, each content to think their own thoughts. Jonathan didn't mention what had upset him at work and he appeared to have forgotten that Karis had been to see Kate as he didn't bring it up, and Karis didn't mention it either as she didn't want to provoke the possible return of his bad humour.

They watched TV for a while, saw the news and opted for an early night as both were working the following day. Karis lay awake for some time, listening to Jon's quiet, even breathing, wishing that she was asleep as well, but when sleep came, it was full of dreams, dreams that made no sense at all and were full of Oliver.

The following evening was much the same as the previous one; Jonathan came into the kitchen, pecked Karis on the cheek, picked up *The Times* and started to read the paper. Karis, feeling tired herself after another very busy day, was not amused. "Another bad day at the office then?" she queried.

"Yep, I guess you could say that," he said, not bothering to raise his eyes from the paper. Oh joy, thought Karis and decided that she would ignore him, getting on with preparing the potatoes and purple sprouting broccoli that they were going to have for dinner. She had already prepared the chicken breasts, splitting them open, putting blue cheese in the cavity and then wrapping them in streaky bacon, all she had to do then was to sauté them in butter, white wine and mushrooms and a spot of single cream and it would be ready in no time. It was one of their favourite meals and she had prepared fresh mango to follow. I just hope it improves his humour, Karis thought.

But it didn't. He ate dinner in almost total silence and didn't comment on what he was eating, only answering her attempts at conversation half-heartedly and with obviously no interest or enthusiasm.

"You didn't ask me about my visit to see Kate, yesterday," she said, wondering even as she spoke whether it was a good idea to bring the subject up. He looked at her, his face composed and registering no emotion. "No. I didn't. I wasn't sure I wanted to know, but you obviously want to tell me, so, was it worth the journey?"

Karis decided to ignore his lack of interest. "I'm glad I went. Kate is still in shock from Oliver's death and is inclined to be tearful but she is trying very hard to get her life back on an even keel and is determined, if she can, to stay at The Pheasants. Obviously, there is no shortage of money." Even as spoke Karis thought it would have been better if she had left that unsaid. However, Jonathan made no comment, just looked at her waiting for her to continue.

"Kate would like me to help out with some cataloguing work. Oliver had a huge collection of books about all sorts of things; art, history, the war, etcetera, and they need to be put in some sort of order before she decides whether to sell them or not. He had one or two first editions which are, I imagine, quite valuable. He also had a large collection of music, LPs, CDs etc. which Kate wants to get rid of too, as she says she has no need of them so that also needs some sorting out as well and possibly selling. And there are also photographs and some pictures that are quite valuable and which cost a fortune in insurance and Kate is not sure about keeping those so they need cataloguing as well." She paused for breath.

"So, she is making you work to pay for your legacy then." Jon's voice was disinterested and showed no emotion. "Are you going to do it?"

"Jonathan! What an awful thing to say. I'm sure Kate doesn't think like that and she said she would pay me anyway. It's got nothing to do with the legacy; in fact, it wasn't mentioned." No way was she going to tell him that Kate had asked her if she had had an affair with

Oliver; the mere thought what his reaction would be gave her the shivers.

"I said I'd think it over and give her my answer in a day or two. Obviously if you have strong objection to my doing the job then I won't do it but I more or less agreed to help out and, for the life of me, I can't see why you should object." Her voice gave away her annoyance.

He looked at her, his eyes expressionless. "It would mean that you were close to him again wouldn't it? Don't tell me you wouldn't enjoy that. I'll never believe that you two weren't lovers."

"Jonathan!" Karis said angrily. "You have no basis, or right to say such a thing. It's mean and untrue. I don't know why you should think it but I am fed up with you being in a bad mood all the time and think it is about time you snapped out of it." Even as she said it she knew that it was a useless thing to say. It was a waste of time to say to someone suffering from depression that they should snap out of it because they just can't do that, but she had hoped that the worst of Jon's illness was behind them and that they were at a stage in their lives when they could get back to enjoying what had once upon a time been a very happy marriage.

"Yeah, I know. You don't have to worry. I'm not about to slide into the abyss again." His tone was reasonable and he even managed a half smile. "One of the guys at work is going through a divorce because his wife has left him for someone else. He is absolutely distraught, unable to cope with doing his job properly and unable to do very much at all. I am not going there."

"I'm sorry to hear that, Jon, but that's not us, is it?" Karis felt sympathy with someone who was in distress but failed to see what it had to do with their problem. "We've been together too long for suspicion to pull us apart. And suspicion is all it is. It's just plain stupid for you to go on thinking the way you are. Surely, together we are stronger than that."

"You would think that way – you've never accepted there was a problem that couldn't be overcome with a bit of tweaking to cover the cracks," John's voice was rising. "You are Mrs bloody Goody Two Shoes, too bloody proper for your own good!"

Karis stared at him in dismay, shattered by his outburst but felt she had to say something in her defence, as he was being so unfair. "Jonathan! That is so untrue. I don't know what to say to you," she finished lamely.

"Then don't bloody well say anything. Just think about it. I'm fed up to the back teeth with always being on the wrong side of an argument. You are always right, you make the decisions and I go along with them. You've made me into a bloody eunuch!"

Karis was horrified, her face wide-eyed with dismay. "Now just a minute, Jonathan. That's below the belt and not fair. I have only taken decisions when you've not been in a position to take them yourself because you haven't been fit or well enough. Before that, either we made them together or you made them – particularly the major ones concerning the house, or schools, or cars or something like that. What on earth has got into you?" Karis felt her blood pressure rising, as well as her voice.

"I've been thinking, that's what's got into me. I think you've been taking me for a ride and, fool that I am, I've been going along with it pretending that everything in the garden was bloody lovely. Well, it's not and I think we should think about a temporary separation to see how we get on."

Karis felt the blood draining from her face. "One minute you say that you are not going there – meaning that you didn't want us to divorce and the next you are suggesting that we separate. Which is it?" Karis's voice was unsteady and loud, filled with fear and dismay.

Jonathan looked at her, his eyes not registering any emotion at all. "I suggest that it would be a good idea if I slept in the spare bedroom while I look for temporary accommodation and we put the house on the market. Now we've done it up it should sell for a few more thousand than we paid for it. We can then split the proceeds and go our separate ways."

Karis stared at him in disbelief. "You haven't just thought that up, have you?" she said. "Obviously, it has been going on in your head for the last few days at least, probably since our holiday. I just can't believe that you are willing to give up all we've got just because you chose to believe something that you have made up in your head. I think at least we should talk it over before we come to any decision and ..." And what? She was so upset she couldn't think straight.

"You're right. I've been considering it since Madeira off and on, and you going over to see Kate was the tipping point," Jonathan said. "A change of direction would be good for both of us. We're at the right age when we've still got time to do something different and make new lives for ourselves."

"Mid-life crisis you mean, only in our case you are making one up because there isn't a real one. Why don't you just say that you want a change? You're not the only man in the world who suddenly decides he wants out in middle-age because he is suddenly bored with his wife and his life," her tone was bitter. She had a sudden thought. "Have you fallen for someone else? Someone you've met at work?"

"No, I haven't and that is not the way I see it either. Christ, Karis! Can't you see it would be good for both of us? We live such humdrum, boring lives it would give both of us a new lease of life."

"Your reasoning doesn't make sense, Jonathan. We've just got ourselves sorted and back on an even keel, health wise and moneywise and we're both in paid employment, although part-time, and are able to pay our bills. We have the house just the way we want it and we are in a position to start doing things together again, holidays, etc. You are not the only one who has been under tremendous strain for the past several years. I feel I am just about coming out of the tunnel and seeing the light and you are sending me right back into another one." Her voice broke. I am not going to cry, she told herself, I am not going to cry. I won't give him the bloody satisfaction.

Jonathan studied his fingernails, unable to meet her eyes.

But Karis wasn't finished yet, determined to try and make him see sense. "I assume from what you say that you don't love me anymore, or least not enough. OK, love is never a given but we've been together for nearly thirty years, doesn't that mean anything to you? Can you just turn your back on me, not to mention Jamie and Joanne, and not have any regrets?"

"That's not fair Karis. Jamie and Joanne have nothing whatsoever to do with it. Of course I'm not turning my back on them and I imagine that I would still see them as much as I do now. They have their own lives to lead and seeing me, or you, is not top of their priorities any more. I imagine that our separating wouldn't mean that much to them, and assuming we are civilised about our situation, there is no reason why we can't get together for family occasions when the need arises."

"Oh! That's all right then; like Joanne getting married you mean?" Karis glared at him. "I think our separating would cause her a great deal of concern not to say upset and your dismissal of its affect on our children is cavalier to say the least." Karis got up from her chair. "I'm going to have a cup of coffee," she said and, unable to stop herself, "would you like one?"

"Yes, please." Jonathan walked into the sitting room, his face set, his mind in turmoil. He hadn't meant to let his thoughts carry him away and he had said things that, although in his mind, he had meant to keep there, at least for the time being. But maybe, now it was out in the open, they should both air their grievances and talk.

They sat in silence drinking their coffee, each lost in their own thoughts, Jonathan defiant and Karis distraught, their easy, comfortable companionship lost, maybe forever.

Karis blinked back tears. Maybe Jonathan had a point. Maybe they had grown complacent and taken each other for granted and she hadn't noticed, content with her life. She was happy with the way things were and he wasn't. Why hadn't he said something before getting to the stage where he didn't want to live with her any longer and given her a chance to make things better between them? How, though? What could she possibly have done that would have been any different? They had weathered the storm when Jonathan had gambled and lost all their money and survived that and his illness; surely they could survive this problem too.

She was suddenly overcome with fatigue and too tired to think any more. Bed was the place to be. At least she could rest her body even if she couldn't sleep. "I'm sorry, Jon. I can't talk now. My mind is in too much of a muddle. The spare bed is made up so you can sleep in there. I'll say goodnight." Automatically, she went towards him for a kiss and then suddenly aware of what she was doing, she hesitated, half smiled at him and then left the room. "I hope you don't sleep at all, all night," she muttered to herself under her breath and then, feeling sheepish and ashamed at the vindictiveness of her feelings, climbed the rest of the stairs to bed. Fat chance of that anyway; Jonathan's sleeping habits meant that he could be hired to sleep for England.

Chapter 14

"One of the chaps at work says I can rent a flat of his for a few months while I look around for something more permanent. I am going to have a look at it on Saturday morning." Jonathan looked at Karis when he spoke, his face serious, no sign of a smile. No change of mind there then. Karis nodded, not trusting herself to speak.

She had managed to get through the last few days by concentrating on what she was doing at any one time and not allowing herself to dwell on thoughts about the end of her marriage as she knew it. She was effectively working on auto-pilot. No one at work knew of her distress, although she was quieter than usual and less inclined to pass the time of day with her colleagues, but they were all so busy that they barely noticed anyway.

She had telephoned Kate to say that she would be happy to help out with the cataloguing and that she would be at The Pheasants in a week's time to start work; it would give her something else to concentrate on. But how was she going to get there if she didn't have a car? Their car was jointly owned like everything else she and Jonathan had but she couldn't work without wheels. Hesitantly, she brought the subject up at breakfast which, like all their meals over the last few days, was being eaten in near silence.

"Would it be OK if I keep using the car for the time being?" It was only about 5 miles to the hospital but it was not on a direct bus route and getting there would be difficult without having her own transport. And getting to The Pheasants would be impossible, except by a very circuitous route which would be both long-winded and tiring and not worth the bother.

"Yes, of course. I can manage without a car on a daily basis but I shall need to use it at the weekend when I go and look at the flat. And I shall want to have my own car again when I move out. We can sell the car when we have sold the house and then get ourselves new ones – I don't mean new ones but you know what I mean." He went back to eating his toast.

"Thanks. I'll ring the estate agent tomorrow and get him to come over and give us an estimate so we can get things moving on the sale."

Jonathan grunted. "That'll be a yes, then?" Karis grinned in spite of herself. When was the last time she had laughed out loud?

Today was Thursday and one of her work-free days. Well, that was a misnomer as she planned to go through the house with the Dyson and generally give it a good blitz before the estate agent came on Saturday afternoon. And there was tidying up to be done in their little patio garden, tying in climbing clematis tendrils, and some weeding between the plants. And then she planned to go over her finances to see whether there was any chance that she might have enough money to be able to buy Jonathan's half of the property. It was just a thought but the more she considered the idea, the more she liked it. Karis hadn't touched the money she had been left by Oliver since she had invested it. It wouldn't have grown very much and there would probably be a penalty to pay but it was in an account in her name so she could do what she wanted with it.

They had only been in the house a relatively short while but in that time she had grown very fond of it and as it was so small it really wouldn't be too much for her on her own, just so long as she could afford it. If only she could get another part-time job that dovetailed in with her present one at the hospital, plus her investment, then she might just be able to afford it.

She looked around her as her thoughts wandered – the decor and the furniture had all been put together with a lot of thought and tender loving care and also with great expectation for their future together. Having survived financial disaster and illness why on earth had it all gone pear-shaped? Karis thought back to the days when Jamie and Joanne had been small children, when they lived in their lovely old rambling, untidy house that was filled with fun and lots of laughter. The thought of telling both of them that she and their father were going to be living apart filled her with foreboding, as she was sure that they would be much more upset about it than Jonathan expected them to be. And they would want to know why of course. Was Jonathan going to tell them that he thought she had had an affair with Oliver?

She suddenly felt very melancholy. They had been so comfortable together, used to each other's foibles and habits and enjoying doing the same things together like going to the theatre and cinema, playing tennis and walking in the countryside and also doing their own things as well so that they were not completely reliant just on each other's company. And their love life had been brilliant too, at least until Jonathan had been ill when medication had caused him to lose his libido.

Maybe she had taken too much for granted, continuing to live along the lines that she thought Jonathan wanted because she wanted it that way herself. He had been protected when ill and she had taken on more of the financial decisions that needed to be taken because at the time it had been essential that she did. Had he resented that, even though he had not been well enough himself to do anything about it?

Karis made herself a cup of coffee and sat out on the patio in the sunshine, appreciating the warmth of the sun. My brain hurts, she thought, with all the thinking and trying to work things out. She would do anything to put things right between them but, it seemed, Jonathan didn't want things put right. For some reason or another he was determined to punish her. But couldn't he see that he wasn't doing himself any favours either as she was sure he wouldn't relish living by himself unless, of course, he really had met someone else and was thinking of starting a relationship. He had denied it but Karis wasn't sure he had been telling her the whole truth.

Karis shivered as a cloud passed in front of the sun temporarily cooling the air. She was torn between trying to save her marriage and just letting Jon get on with his plans as if she didn't really care what he did; there was such a thing as pride, though, and hers was being severely tested.

It was just so completely out of character for Jonathan to go off at the deep end. Placid and gentle by nature, it had always taken a lot for him to lose his temper; he preferred to look at things objectively and from all angles in an effort to get things right before making any judgement. But recently his personality had taken on subtle changes and he was no longer predictable and the Jonathan she knew and had fallen in love with.

Karis sighed deeply. She had decided that it was worthwhile trying to talk Jonathan round to giving their marriage one last chance. She would talk to him about it when he got home from work and if he was still determined to leave then she would accept his decision and start making plans for herself for the future, even though the mere thought of what that entailed filled her with sadness and not a little dread. What on earth was she going to do with herself?

Chapter 15

"Joanne is coming over to see us on Sunday. I spoke to her today and she said she would be here, just her, not with Lee, about 12ish and she would like some lunch. I assume you haven't got any other plans and that is OK with you?" Karis's voice was brisk and business like.

"Yes, of course. That's fine. I shall look forward to seeing her," Jon spoke from behind the newspaper. "Did she say why Lee isn't coming?"

"No. She didn't. Well not exactly anyway. Something about overtime but no doubt she will tell us when she gets here." Karis put the supper on the table and sat down. "Supper is ready."

Jonathan came to the table. "Fillet steak. Lovely! We're pushing the boat out a bit aren't we?" and he picked up his knife and fork with enthusiasm. At least he still enjoyed good food, Karis thought, having gone to some trouble in cooking something especially nice for their supper.

They ate in silence which, unlike in the past when they always talked to each other about what had happened to them that day or discussed local or topical news, was not now unusual.

"I wondered whether you had had any second thoughts about leaving me. With Joanne coming on Sunday I would like to get things straight between us before we mention anything to her about what is happening to us."

Jonathan ate the last mouthful of steak and asparagus and put his knife and fork down before looking up. "No. As far as I am concerned, nothing has changed since we last talked about me leaving. I still want to make a clean break, even though I have to concede that you are a very good cook. That was very nice thank you." His tone was mater-of-fact.

"Glad you liked it. No doubt you are looking forward to cooking for yourself. Would you like some strawberries and ice cream?"

Karis waited for his reply which was a "Yes, please," before getting up from the table. Just how formal can you get, she thought, hoping for an appreciative smile by way of thanks.

They were drinking coffee when Karis decided that she would make one last effort. "Jonathan. Please reconsider what you are planning to do. I don't want us to break-up, I shall miss you dreadfully and I am willing to do anything to make you change your mind and stay with me."

Jonathan looked at her, his face showing no emotion at all but obviously looking for the right words to say to her. "It's not as if I haven't given it a lot of thought," he said, "in fact I've thought of little else for the past several weeks so it is unlikely that I am going to change my mind now. No, I think it will be good for both of us – new surroundings, new friends and a new lease of life. My health is much better these days and I feel I can do very well looking after myself with no one else restricting my life and what I want to do and no encumbrances."

Encumbrances! So that was what he thought she was. Karis was taken aback. Dismayed and then furious. If that was the way he felt there was no point in trying to change his mind and she was not going to eat any more humble pie in order to try and get him to change his mind. He could just sod off!

135

"Fine! That's it then. At least I know where I stand. We both get on with our lives – separately." Disappointed and feeling rebuffed, Karis stood up and started clearing the table.

Jonathan went off in the car on Saturday morning to view the flat. It was not far away but he said that he wanted to have the car as he had something else he wanted to do; he didn't say what. He was whistling softly to himself as he went out the door for all the world as if he was going to a game of football with his friends and not to start the process of bringing his marriage to Karis to an end.

The flat – sitting room, bedroom, small bathroom and even smaller kitchen – was the ground floor of a semi-detached house in a road that was lined on either side with lime trees. Jonathan was not too bothered about the colour of the walls or the furniture but he made sure that the bathroom was in good working order and the kitchen contained the necessary cooker, fridge and washing machine. There was also a range of cleaning equipment and a vacuum cleaner and ironing board housed in a cupboard under the stairs which he gave scant attention to; his thoughts on living on his own hadn't got as far as doing anything other than cooking himself dinner in the evening and maybe putting the washing machine on. There would be plenty of time to think about anything else that may be needed doing when he had actually moved in.

His friend, Tom Wood, waited for him outside in the garden. He had already told Jon what the rent would be per month which Jon considered reasonable and within his price capability, although, until the house was sold, would make things tight with not much left over for extras.

"Thanks for waiting, Tom. The flat is fine and will suit me very well. When can I move in?"

"Any time you like but just to tidy things up, how about the beginning of next month? I'll have my solicitor draw up a six month contract and you can then move in. I'm pleased it suits you, just sorry that you are moving in on your own. No chance of you mending bridges with your wife then?"

Jonathan hadn't said anything to Tom other than that he and Karis had decided, amicably, to part and to go their different and separate ways.

"Not at the moment, no. I think it will be better for both of us to have a complete break, although we shall have family get togethers from time to time. Now, having sorted out the flat, how about that pint of beer?" It was time to get back into doing a few more 'men' things with his friends.

The house was looking especially pretty when the estate agent came to do the evaluation and the garden had plenty of colour in it to make it look very appealing. Karis was experiencing very mixed feelings. Obviously, she wanted them to get a good price for the property if they were both leaving but, if she was to continue with her plan to buy Jonathan's half, then obviously the lower the price the better it would be for her.

The estate agent was very impressed with the improvements and decorating they had done to the interior of the house and said that he thought that they would have no trouble at all in selling it. "It is all looking very tidy," he said, "and with the first-time buyers coming along again, you should have no trouble at all in getting a quick sale. He talked in positives all the time, a kind of estate agent gobble-de-gook that Karis thought was way over the top and which often put

137

far too high an expectation on people being able to sell their houses. However, he was a professional so she would have to trust his judgement and he should know what he was talking about.

He quoted a figure that was £10,000 more than they had paid for it and considering they had only been in the property for such a comparatively short time, Jonathan was very pleased; Karis quietly less so.

"Shall I go ahead and get the photographs and details ready for the press?"

Karis hesitated and looked at Jonathan. "We'll talk it over this evening and come back to you tomorrow," she said, "there are one or two things I want to discuss with my husband before we make the final decision."

Jonathan gave her a quizzical look wondering what she was talking about but said nothing. As far as he was concerned, they had done all the talking and it was now time for some action.

Karis closed the door on the estate agent and turned to face Jon. "I've had some thoughts," she said and then hesitated, not quite knowing how she was going to put it to him. "I wondered whether I might just be able to buy your half of the property and stay here. It would make sense, I think." Her voice wobbled a bit betraying her nervousness at discussing her thoughts with him. She took a deep breath, "And it would save us the expense of employing an estate agent. All we would need would be for a solicitor to draw up the necessary paperwork. What do you think?"

"I think I can see the advantages of having some ill-gotten gains! Bloody hell! What else have you been secretly planning? I think you should at least have had the decency to talk about this with me before we had the estate agent round." He was clearly angry, his face flushed.

"I'm sorry, Jonathan, but I only thought about the possibility very recently so there hasn't been any time to discuss it with you. And really it doesn't make too much difference to you, as you will still get half the value of the house anyway. The fact that I may still be living here instead of moving into a flat is surely neither here nor there since you've chosen to move out anyway. It doesn't really make any difference to you, just as long as you get your share." She didn't add that he could come back at any time he wanted to; clearly, that wasn't an option that appealed to him. "And anyway, at the moment it is just a thought. I will have to talk to the bank and see whether I can stretch the finances to be able to afford to do it.

"And you haven't told me what you thought about the flat. Is it suitable?" Karis tried to sound interested. Jonathan had arrived back at the house just before the estate agent had arrived and there had been no time for them to discuss it.

"Yes, it's fine. Basic, but then, what do I need? Tom says I can move in at the beginning of next month and I shall sign a six month lease which will give me time to assess the market with a view to possibly buying a small flat. And if I get more work that will help too, so, I have lots to look forward to." He went on, enthusiasm building, "And if we get the price the estate agent thinks we will, that will be a bonus." He paused, brow furrowed. "I went for a beer with Tom to the sports club after looking at the flat and he says he will propose my membership of the club if I am interested. They have lots of facilities and it would be cheaper than the gym I usually go to. So everything seems to be falling into place."

He sat down in the sitting room and picked up the paper. "What's for dinner?"

"I've no idea," Karis replied. "I haven't thought. Have you?"

Jonathan looked at her, his eyes puzzled. "No, of course I haven't. You always take care of the food."

"Precisely! I always look after the food. Well, that is something you are going to have to start thinking about for yourself now, isn't it? Food doesn't just cook itself. It has to be planned, chosen or selected at the shop and it is then prepared and cooked. Strangely, it doesn't just happen all by itself. Cooking now and again when you feel like is not going to be enough from now on if you want to eat and stay healthy." I'd better not go on, she thought. He's probably got the message by now.

And then, feeling rather mean, she relented. "How about we have fish and chips from the local shop? It is Saturday night after all."

Chapter 16

"Hello Sweetheart. How are you?" Jonathan greeted his daughter, giving her a bear-hug and kissing her cheek. "It's lovely to see you. Why haven't you brought that young man with you?"

"Hi Dad, it's lovely to see you as well. And Mum," she said as she turned to hug her mother. "Lee has gone up to Chester to see his parents. They have sold their shop and are getting ready to go off on their travelling and they wanted Lee to help out with a few things and also to update him on what they need him to do for them while they are away. And also, he and I have decided that things were getting a bit too intense and serious between us so, what with him having just finished taking his finals and feeling like a complete break from me, work and everything...well, we haven't been seeing quite so much of each other lately. It's for the best I think. For both of us." Her weak smile and watery eyes belied her words and gave away her secret feelings of hurt.

"It's nothing to worry about, though, so don't. We're still seeing each other only not just as often and I'm sure it will all work out OK, eventually, one way or the other." Her crestfallen face was a picture of unhappiness.

Karis put a cup of coffee at Joanne's elbow. "I don't expect that a little bit of a breather for both of you will do any harm," she said, trying to put a positive angle on the situation, "and, in fact, it might even be a good thing in a way. He'll come back saying how much he has missed you and appreciating you even more." She patted her daughter's arm and gave her a reassuring smile, fervently hoping that that would be the case as she liked Lee very much and thought he would make a lovely son-in-law.

"So how is work going for you, Jo? Are you still as busy as ever? And are you enjoying it as much?" It was necessary for her to know that her daughter was at least happy in her work, even if her personal life had gone slightly awry.

Joanne's face brightened immediately. "Yes, I am, Mum. Something new happens every day and it is never boring and while people are hell-bent on keeping fit, there will always be injuries of one kind or another for me to work on." She laughed, "Funny that. Something of a paradox but it keeps me busy. If only people realised that warming-up and warming-down is essential instead of starting off exercising at full tilt. But where would I be without them? So, yes, I am happy that I am doing my job and not some boring thing stuck in an office doing routine stuff every day."

She drank some coffee and looking at each of them in turn asked how they both were. She wasn't really particularly interested, being more concerned with her own problems, but she felt that she had to be polite and ask anyway. Her parents were always all right.

Karis looked at Jonathan. Was he going to say anything, or would he leave it to her to answer? Silly question; he would leave it to her, of course.

"Well, actually darling," she started, "we are glad you've come today because we have got something to tell you. Dad has decided that he would like to have some space and in order to give him that space he wants us to separate and to live independently. Do different things with different people. Sort of re-charge his batteries." She hesitated as she was watching Joanne's face and it was registering increasing alarm.

142

"You are joking of course?" Joanne's tone was bordering on the hysterical. This couldn't be her two loving parents about to go their own separate ways. "How can you possibly do that? Or even think such a thing? You've been together for ever and I don't think for one minute you could possibly live apart and be happy. Have you gone mad? Please tell me you don't mean it?" She was looking tearful again, her face a picture of concern.

Jonathan thought it was about time he added his contribution to the conversation, Karis having laid the blame squarely at his door. "People change, Joanne, as they get older. We've had a very good run for our money and now it's time to explore other avenues while we've still got time."

"You are talking in bloody clichés, Dad. While you've still got time! What on earth are you talking about? You are both in the prime of life! Surely you don't have to separate? You can still do anything you want to while still being together. How long has this stupid idea been going on for? I must say you've completely shattered me. Yours was the marriage that was held up as the template. Now what am I going to do?"

Trust the young to think of how the situation would affect them, Karis thought as she tried to calm her daughter down, alarmed at her distress and reaction to the news of her parent's imminent separation. "We're still friends, darling, we haven't fallen out." That's not really true, she thought to herself. "We shall still see you as much as ever, although probably at different times and we can certainly be together on family occasions like, for instance, birthdays or if either you or Jamie ever decide to get married. Things like that."

143

"Have you told Jamie yet?" Joanne asked. "And what is going to happen about Christmas? What are we going to do then?" Her mind was in a whirl. She had come home for the day so that she could tell her parents all about her current problems and they had turned things on their head and were telling her about theirs. "It's just not fair and it is just plain stupid. Both of you should have more sense." She blew her nose loudly.

"This is not something that we planned to happen, Joanne, it just has, and we're not exactly unique are we? It happens to thousands of couples all the time." Karis felt she had to try and justify what was happening and to get Joanne to see things from their perspective instead of just her own.

"I am hoping to be able to scrape up enough money to be able to buy Dad's half of the property and stay here and Dad will look for somewhere else to buy with his half of the proceeds. For the time being he will move into a friend's flat and we will then both get on with our lives. It won't really make too much difference to you and, anyway, you have lots to look forward to yourself; thank goodness you enjoy your job. And no, we haven't told Jamie yet. It's not an easy thing to do on the telephone so we are hoping that he might come home for a day soon so we can update him then."

Jamie worked for an advertising agency as a graphic designer in London and came home rarely, being very busy all week in the office and even busier at the weekends having fun and, they gathered from what he said, living life to the full. Their contact with him was not much more than a fortnightly telephone call in the name of duty when he was always cheerful, delighted to talk to them but with never a minute to spare, a situation that Karis found entirely to be expected with a 28 year old man in the prime of life. Karis would suggest a visit next time he called or maybe Joanne would mention it when they were next in contact. Their relationship was close, always had been. They had been the best of friends as children when Jamie, as an elder brother had always been very protective of his younger sister and their friendship had grown and remained strong into adulthood.

"It all sounds so very un-family like – the sort of thing that happens to other families, not mine. Why can't things ever stay the same?" Joanne wailed, blowing her nose again, still distressed and unhappy.

Sunday lunch for the three of them was short on conversation and long on silences, despite Karis and Jonathan both making an effort to keep the conversation going. Joanne was clearly shocked and was not going to be easily cajoled into their usual familiar easy togetherness with lots of chatter and laughs. She remained stubbornly quiet, her face serious as if she had the weight of the world on her shoulders. Even the roast pork and apple pie failed to bring a smile to her face.

Joanne ate slowly, inwardly digesting what she had been told and trying to make sense of it all. Never in a million years would she have expected her parents to separate; they had always seemed so in tune with each other, even when her dad had been ill. Not that she had ever given them much thought to be honest; they were just there and she had completely taken them for granted. They would always be there, wouldn't they, especially when she needed them which she did right now. She wanted to tell them she was worried that perhaps Lee wouldn't come back to her, that he would get used to being without her and find that he didn't need her any more. But now she didn't feel that she could worry them about her fears as they had something a great deal more worrying to think about.

"Have you made any plans for a holiday with Lee? You haven't been away for a long time and you could probably do with a break somewhere warm." Karis was still grasping at straws trying to get Joanne to say something.

A feeling of hopelessness suddenly came over her. What was she doing, trying to act as if everything was OK when she felt like going into a corner and screaming as loud as she could that life was bloody awful at times? She glanced at Jonathan, eyes downcast and busy clearing his plate, seemingly oblivious to both Joanne's and her distress.

"No. No plans at the moment, although we did vaguely think that we might go away at Christmas for a week or so for a complete break, perhaps somewhere snowy. Whether we shall or not depends on duty rotas etc. and we shall have to wait and see what happens. A lot depends on Lee's results and what he has to do for his parents."

"Well, then. That would take care of your Christmas, darling, wouldn't it?" Karis smiled at her daughter. "You see, it's just as I said, nothing stays the same and you wouldn't have to worry about having to visit your parents would you, so that would be a plus for you."

And what the hell will I do? Christmas was never, ever going to be the same again and, frankly, she couldn't bear thinking about it. The conversation gradually lapsed with none of them willing, or able, to make an effort to keep it going.

Chapter 17

The cataloguing was going well. Karis had decided to tackle the CDs and LPs first as she felt it was unlikely that Kate would want to keep more than a few and this assumption proved correct. Oliver's musical taste had been eclectic. He had been particularly fond of both jazz and opera and his collection of both was extensive, including a complete set of Maria Callas's LPs, but he had also collected music from films and shows and then there were the classical LPs – Beethoven and Mozart, some Tchaikovsky and Rachmaninov. Occasionally, Karis played an LP on the turntable while she worked, thinking that sitting down for half an hour a day just listening to a favourite piece of music should be compulsory for everyone – time to relax and do nothing, just appreciate the heritage of someone else's genius. Fat chance of that ever happening, she thought.

Occasionally, Kate would come into the study and sit and listen to the music with Karis, both women quiet and thoughtful, but Kate seldom stayed for more than a few minutes, as she didn't want to interrupt Karis's work. She did, however, indicate that her personal preference was for music from the shows, often joining in singing some of the songs and melodies with a voice that, had it been trained, might very well have been very good indeed, and Karis told her so.

"I always wanted to go on the stage when I was a girl and my mother went as far as writing to several drama schools when I was about 17 and very keen on a career as an actress. However, my father didn't like the idea at all as he was old-fashioned about daughters going on the stage, and since he would have had to finance me, I'm afraid my hopes of becoming a recognised singer or actress died the death early on. Probably just as well, although I often wonder if I would have been any good." Kate smiled as she spoke. "No point in thinking back about what might have been as nothing is going to change it." She got up from where she had been perching on the arm of a chair and said, "I'll get us some coffee."

During the few weeks that Karis had been working on the cataloguing, the two women had grown to like each other and Kate looked forward to Karis's visits. Gradually, her grief and loneliness had subsided and apart from occasional lapses when she was at a loss for something to do and she indulged in a bout of melancholy she began to think that perhaps life was worth living after all. Her painting classes were proving very beneficial and they had a definite calming effect on her and, if she fully applied herself, her water colours were improving and were often very good indeed.

"So I think that I'll just keep some of the music from the shows and a few classical LPs and the odd aria or two and get rid of the rest," Kate was thinking out loud. "I'll ask the girls if they want any of them and then when they've taken what they want they can be sold, or given away to the charity shops as I don't suppose there is much of a market for LPs or CDs for that matter. I'm sure Oliver wouldn't mind."

Kate seldom mentioned Oliver. At first when Karis started her visits his name never came up but now that they had formed a closer relationship, Kate occasionally brought him into their conversations again and she was able to mention him without her eyes filling with tears. But whether he was mentioned or not, he still seemed to be a presence in the house and both women, independently and quietly to themselves, acknowledged that he still, to a small degree, influenced both of them.

"I'll start on the books on my next visit Kate, I'm looking forward to that," Karis said. She didn't add that she and Oliver had often had discussions about favourite authors, their preferences mostly differing but occasionally they agreed with each other. When they disagreed, debates would follow, often developing into lively arguments about merits or otherwise of particular authors; what wasn't at odds was that they both loved to read and considered the time spent occupied with a good book was time not wasted but well spent.

One of the books that they both loved was *The Cruel Sea* by Nicholas Monsarrat, which they considered had everything: authority, love, integrity, heartache; all human nature was there. And it was written in beautiful English, too. What more could you ask for?

Karis had already been in contact with some local book shops and had started to learn a bit about values and the possibility of selling some of the books but unless a book was rare, sought after or a first edition there wasn't much chance of making much money from them. However, that wasn't really the object of the exercise. First and foremost, the books were to be put in order and catalogued to see precisely what there was there and Kate could then decide what she wanted to do with them.

The sky was grey, with low scudding clouds when Karis left The Pheasants to drive home, some small sleety flakes beginning to fall. The weather forecast was not good with very cold winds sweeping in all over the country from the north for the next few days. Well it was winter so foul weather wasn't entirely unexpected.

Karis had enjoyed the morning, feeling that she was getting somewhere with the job in hand and looking forward to tackling the next phase of her job. She was sure she would be able to make a good job of sorting out all the books but she had reservations about the paintings and she would speak to Kate about that when she next visited in two weeks time. Her knowledge of art was only rudimentary and she thought that after an initial exercise sifting and sorting, an expert was going to be required to help finish the job, unless Kate decided that she would select what she liked and then just sell the rest to a reputable dealer.

She was feeling mellow, pleased that Kate was beginning to show signs of getting over Oliver's death and that the relationship between them was pleasant without being overly friendly. She was pleased, too, that she had an alternative job to do, one that was interesting without being too taxing, as she had not been able to find another part-time one that would dove-tail with her three days at the hospital although heaven knew she had tried to find extra work.

After she and Jonathan went their separate ways she had managed to scrape together enough money to buy his share of the house, with the help of a small loan from the bank, but she often had doubts about whether it had been an altogether sensible thing to do as she was consequently always short of money. It was a fact that she kept to herself, though, as she didn't want anyone else to know she was finding life on a shoestring difficult, most of all, Jonathan. She could hear her mother saying in her ear that she had made her bed, so she had better lie on it! So that was what she would do.

She sighed. She didn't really have any regrets about her decision as she had her home which she loved and which required very little work from her to keep it looking nice; but she missed Jonathan more than she thought she would – his sense of humour which mirrored her own, his understanding of her moods and the way he could take up and finish one of her sentences as he knew exactly what she was thinking and what she was going to say.

She seldom saw him now and on the odd occasion when he had rung and said he was calling round for a book or something that he needed, they had been polite to each other as if they were distant cousins who seldom met and were passing the time of day with each other, and he had escaped as quickly as he could. Back to what? More of the same? His own solitary company, maybe watching TV, reading books and having the odd beer now and again with his friends?

He never volunteered any information about his life and she pretended not to care or to be bothered about what he was doing. What if he said he had a girlfriend? What would she do then – pretend to be pleased for him while all the time feeling sick with jealousy? Pride kept her from asking. He had elected to leave her and she wasn't going to beg him to come back to her, even though she felt distraught each time when he left.

I'll get over it, she told herself. It's not the end of the world. Nobody's died. But the feeling of despair persisted. Try as she might, she just couldn't shake it off. Just stop thinking about him, she told herself, you know it makes you miserable. Think, instead, of the fact that when you get home you can do exactly what you want to do, have a bath, do some skipping – where did that come from? - eat whatever you want without a second thought for anyone else, watch any TV programme you feel like without considering any other person's preferences, have supper in bed, read a book, listen to music...I could go on and on, she thought.

She smiled to herself as she drove the car into the village. She was nearly home now and was feeling distinctly more positive about her lonely life. That felt much better. All she had to do was think positive!

Chapter 18

In spite of her own good advice, the next morning Karis's feeling of gloom persisted. She arrived at work and walked into her office still trying to put a smile on her face. She said good morning to all the staff and to Jill and Angela, as she usually did, but then examined her in tray and started work without adding the usual pleasantries that she would normally do. As usual, there was plenty of work to get on with that would keep her busy for the next few hours.

She was half way into a very lengthy report when Dr Matthews put his head round the door and asked if she could come to his room after his morning tour of the wards. She nodded and, barely stopping to acknowledge his request, continued feeding the computer.

At just before 11 am she knocked on Dr Matthew's door and went in. As usual, he was writing, filling in a form with his comments, his head supported by his left hand. He continued writing for a moment then looked up, smiled and put his pen down. "Sorry, Karis. There was a thought in my head that I wanted to get down on paper before I forgot it. All done now." He sat back in his chair. "Please sit down."

He appeared relaxed but was looking at her with concern on his face. "What's wrong, Karis?"

She was completely taken by surprise. She hadn't thought why he might want to see her, assuming that it was just something to do with extra work which was the usual reason he asked to see her. "Nothing is wrong. Nothing at all. Why do you ask?" She tried to make her voice sound as relaxed and normal as possible and her face unconcerned, but not quite succeeding with either.

"It's part of my job to watch people and, although you are an employee of the hospital and therefore outside my remit, I've noticed lately that you haven't been your usual bright and sunny self and I wondered if there was anything I could do to help. You're not feeling ill are you? You certainly don't look ill but you have been causing me concern because if there is one person who can lift the spirits with a smile, it is you. And that smile has been missing for some little while now."

Karis attempted a smile to belie his words. "I'm sorry, Dr Matthews. I know I've been a bit out of sorts lately and, try as I might, I haven't been able to rise above it, but I didn't realise it was so obvious. Sorry." She briefly considered bluffing it out and not saying anything at all, pretending it was just 'one of those things' but she decided that she had nothing to lose and that honestly in this case was probably the best policy.

"My husband left me a few months ago. At first I thought he was just making a gesture of independence but he is showing every sign of actually enjoying himself and it has left me feeling absolutely bereft – desolate even. He had a breakdown three years ago and he was unfit to work for two years but since he has been well enough to work again, he has been a changed man, more independent and determined to get on again. And somehow, for some reason I can't put my finger on, our relationship has changed as well." Talking about it made Karis's throat ache holding back the tears that were threatening to flow. She sniffed and then blew her nose as Dr Matthews handed her a tissue.

"So. It's not nothing is it? In fact, it's something big and very important." Dr Matthews smiled at her.

"There must be something I can do to help, even if it is just to listen to you when you need to have a grumble. I can understand what is going on in your husband's head, he is basically reasserting himself and trying to prove to himself that he can manage on his own without being looked after by anyone else; it is a natural process, and although I can't predict how it will all turn out, the chances are that he will gradually come to realise that having a loving partner to share his life with again, will take over from his current wish to do things on his own."

"So he isn't being particularly unusual then?" Karis needed more reassurance.

"No. Not really. But then, everyone is different and, consequently, predictable behaviour is not a given." Dr Matthews smiled at her reassuringly. "Again, the chances are that he will come to his senses after a while and wonder what on earth he is doing, although it may take a little more time yet. My advice to you would be to just keep your chin up and, if you can, be your usual cheerful self whenever you see him."

Karis felt her anxieties lift a little and she returned Dr Matthews smile. "Thank you for taking the time and trouble to listen to me," she said. "You've no idea how much better you've made me feel." She stood up, an uncertain smile replacing the totally blank expression she had on her face when coming into the room.

"Actually, I've just had a thought," Dr Matthews said. "Do you like live theatre? And if you do, would you like to come with me to the opening night of a play at the Sheridan Theatre in a week's time. You'd be doing me an enormous favour if you would. I've been given two tickets for a play plus a threat of ex-communication by my family if I don't turn up. My nephew is appearing in the play in what I can only describe as a small part, but to him it is very important, as it is to my sister and her husband so I really must make an effort to go. Please say you will come." Dr Matthews' voice was coaxing her to say yes.

"That sounds lovely and I do love live theatre. I'll check the calendar when I get home and let you know tomorrow. I'm pretty certain that I've nothing on then – it would be very unusual if I had. I really must get out more. Thank you, Dr Matthews, for thinking of me."

"Please call me Bill," he grinned at her "At least when we are out of work environs and, may I call you Karis, Mrs Fielden? It is an unusual name. Has it any connection with Egypt by any chance?"

"Yes, it has – was that an educated guess or did you know? My parents had a holiday there years ago, fell in love with the country and everything about it and decided to remember it by naming me Karis which, apparently, means grace and beauty in that country and, I think, in Greece. It's a difficult name to live up to but, fortunately, most people don't know what it means which is a relief as it rather lets me off the hook from trying to achieve either."

"It is unusual but it is pretty and I think it suits you. So Karis and Bill it is, and hopefully you will be able to confirm you are free for our theatre date next week – I shall look forward to it with you as my companion instead of going along reluctantly as a duty."

The rest of the day passed quickly; the work somehow flowed more easily and it seemed no time at all before it was 'packing up for the day time' and for the evening to begin. Karis switched off her computer, said a cheery goodnight to her colleagues and drove home, for once feeling more in tune with her life and not completely at odds with the world. And also, just for a change, she had something to look forward to. I wonder if the play will be any good, she pondered? But more to the point, what would Bill Matthews be like as a date? Stop that, she told herself, he was obviously just being kind to her, but it still made her feel better about herself and not quite so down-in-the-mouth as she had been lately.

Chapter 19

The 'feel better' feeling didn't last long. It was a Friday evening, the weekend stretched before her – empty with nothing planned to do at all. Karis automatically went into her usual routine – change out of her work clothes and into leisure pants and comfortable top, pour glass of wine, sit and contemplate and digest what her day had brought and decide what to do to pass the time over the Saturday and Sunday. OK, she said to herself, do something different for a change – don't just sit there! But after a few minutes contemplation, she got up, poured herself another glass of wine and decided that she would let the weekend take care of itself.

The wine was particularly delicious. Was this because it was a better quality than usual or perhaps because she was feeling less strung-out, tired and fed up at the end of a busy week and her taste buds were detecting less of her own bile? She laughed, thinking that she was being stupid. But maybe it was also because she had something different to do and look forward to next week. She couldn't remember the last time she went to either live theatre to see a play or even to the cinema to see a film as it was not something she wanted to do on her own, preferring to spend her evenings at home.

Her thoughts automatically turned to Bill Matthews – she knew his name was Bill, of course, but since starting work at the hospital, she had kept to the formal way of speaking to him, as well as the other doctors, as that way it kept things on a business level and she hadn't ever thought of calling him by his first name. Bill. She decided that it suited him; dependable, reliable and someone to whom you could tell your innermost troubles to and know that there would be no judgement or recrimination in return; just good advice.

Karis finished her glass of wine and decided that she would have another, just because she could with no one asking if it was wise? It probably wasn't but what the hell! She opened the freezer and examined the contents, largely filled with a selection of good quality ready meals, selected a fish pie to put in the oven for later, thinking as she did so that she would get some fresh meat when she went to the shops tomorrow and would cook something for herself on Sunday. It was about time she stopped being so lazy and started cooking again instead of taking the easy option all the time.

While enjoying the wine and giving scant attention to the news on the TV as she did so, Karis decided that she would go into town tomorrow and try and get her hair cut, maybe have a look at clothes – when did she last do that? – And possibly have some lunch if she felt hungry enough. A break from work, domestic chores and a humdrum routine would be good for her; the usual household chores could go hang! Meantime, she would give Joanne a ring to see how she was and maybe she would like to meet her for some lunch if she wasn't too busy and could spare the time.

The sun was shining next morning, albeit somewhat weakly and with not a lot of warmth. Karis dressed with a little more care than she usually did when she was going to work and with regard to the coolness of the day - black trousers and ankle boots, polo cashmere sweater in cream and lime green jacket. She gave her hair a quick brush and she was ready to go.

The first hair salon she went into was unable to help her, being fully booked for the day, but when she came to the second one, the receptionist said they could squeeze her in if she didn't mind waiting for ten minutes or so. She didn't. It gave her time to ponder whether she really wanted to get her hair cut, having worn it either jaw length or longer for several years but the stylist thought it a good idea and said it would take ten years off her age, showing her a style that she thought would be particularly flattering.

An hour and a bit later and considerably lighter in her purse, Karis looked at herself in the mirror and decided that the stylist was right. Her hair had been cut in an Audrey Hepburn style and she looked completely different, definitely younger and very much smarter. What will Jonathan think? she wondered, her thoughts automatically turning to him before anyone else. He had always preferred her to have her hair long and had said that it was her lovely auburn hair that had attracted him to her in the first place; he wouldn't like it at all she decided. However, it didn't matter a jot what he thought as he no longer had any influence over her and she was pretty sure that Joanne would give it her approval.

Joanne was to meet her at one o'clock at a little bistro in the High Street having said to Karis that she had no appointments with clients for the Saturday morning but that she wouldn't be able to stay for too long in the afternoon as she was going to an Amateur Dramatic Society that evening to see about joining and she had a few things she needed to do before she went.

Karis had been pleased to hear Joanne's news as it was something that she knew would be good for her having enjoyed acting in her school plays and it would, if she joined, give her a chance to meet some new friends and help to fill her spare time when Lee was working or busy and couldn't get to see her. Karis was hopeful that the news from Joanne regarding Lee would be better than it had been last time she had seen her.

Joanne arrived just after their agreed meeting time to find Karis sitting at a table in the window, watching the world go by while glancing at the menu and trying to make up her mind whether she was hungry enough for a proper lunch or she would just have a snack. Some of the dishes on offer sounded delicious.

"Hello, Mum." She bent to kiss her on the cheek. "You look great and your hair is super! It looks really lovely. Has it just been done? I don't think I have ever seen you with short hair before, have I?" She kissed Karis on the other cheek and plonked herself down in the nearest chair. "It really suits you. Are you pleased with it?"

"Yes I am. And no, I don't think you have. I was probably still at school the last time it was this short. Thanks, Joanne. I must admit it's a bit of a shock when I catch sight of myself and it is going to take some getting used to but I think I shall like it once I do, and it will certainly be easier to manage and not take so long to dry. Lots of positives there," she grinned happily at her daughter, "and I am all for those.

"I was just wondering what your father would think of it but since I barely see him these days, it doesn't really matter what he thinks does it? Anyway, enough of my hair – are you hungry? Apparently they do a very nice wild mushroom risotto here, which I think I am going to go for, how about you?"

They chatted away, happy to be in each other's company and while they waited for their food, Karis asked Joanne about the Amateur Dramatic Society she had mentioned.

"One of my clients told me about it. She is a member and she said they were looking to recruit new members. Apparently they put on two plays, or shows, mostly plays, a year and always need new members. They use the local community hall which has very good facilities: stage, dressing rooms off, kitchen etc. and everyone mucks in with painting scenery, providing costumes and props etc. and it is very much an 'all hands on' outfit. Sounds fun. Of course, they are always short of men so I thought I would mention it to Lee to see if he would be interested in joining too, once I've been and seen what it is all about and maybe joined." Joanne's voice gave away her enthusiasm. She hadn't been involved with amateur dramatics since she had left school, having been fully occupied with and giving her priority to becoming a qualified physiotherapist.

"You are still seeing Lee, then? I wondered whether you had both had a change of heart." Karis didn't want to appear to be too interested in her daughter's personal life but she couldn't help wanting to know what was going on and she had thought that Lee had been an almost perfect partner for Joanne.

"Yes, we are still seeing each other and no, we haven't had a change of heart. Or at least I haven't. We see each other a couple of times a week which is fine for both of us as we both have a lot of work on. Of course there is a chance that Lee will move to another hospital soon, after he has finished his first year and I don't know what will happen then. Keep my fingers crossed and hope for the best, I guess, but I don't want him to think that I can't possibly live without him – even if I can't. Meantime, we still enjoy each other's company, we've just cooled it a bit, that's all."

Joanne finished her plate of prawn salad. "That was good. Are we having pudding?"

Karis smiled at her, "I should think so. It's not often I get the chance to treat you to lunch so we'll make the most of it. And I've got something to tell you, too. Dr Matthews has asked me to go to the theatre with him next Friday and I've said yes. I can't remember the last time I went out for an evening. What do you think about that?"

Joanne stared at her mother. "I don't honestly know what I think. My mother going out with a strange man! What is he like? Good looking, fun to be with?"

Joanne didn't want her mother to know that she was slightly perturbed with her announcement; it wasn't that she disapproved or didn't want her to go out on a date, but it was not what she was expecting to hear. Surely her mum and dad would both see sense and get back together again soon. She had always thought that it was just a temporary gap in their relationship while her father got back to full health and employment, found his feet so to speak without being constantly under her mother's beady eye, did things for himself instead of always relaying on someone else, but if her mother started going out with another man goodness knows where that would end up. She wasn't sure she approved and would need time to think things over.

Karis could almost read what her daughter was thinking. "Don't worry, Joanne. It's just a one off. Bill Matthews is a very nice, well-mannered man who will not, I am sure, put a foot wrong so you've no need for concern. And I shall look forward to enjoying a nice visit to the theatre for a change with a nice companion instead of being on my own. Believe me, it gets very miserable at times."

"Yes, of course, Mum. It hasn't exactly been easy for you recently I know. Just make sure you are home and in bed by 10.30!" They smiled at each other, both enjoying the joke.

Chapter 20

Karis was not due to go to The Pheasants on the Thursday of the following week so she spent the day in a domestic whirl and then pondered the question of what she should wear to the theatre on the Friday evening, something smart but casual perhaps. She couldn't make up her mind whether she was looking forward to going out or not, it was such a long time since she had done anything socially with anyone other than with her husband or the family.

Karis didn't see Dr Matthews on the Friday – she still thought of him that way at work – until about four in the afternoon, he having been busy attending a clinic at a half-way house. He came into the office and, seeing Karis's two office companions at their desks and wanting to have a private word with her, asked her to come to his office.

"Everything OK for this evening? I'll pick you up at 6.30 and we can then have a drink before curtain up at 7.30 – it shouldn't take us longer than twenty minutes or so to get there, although finding somewhere to park might be a problem. I just need to know how to get to your house – I know approximately where it is, just not exactly."

Karis gave him instructions and the post-code in case he wanted to use his GPS. "Haven't got one," he said. "I'm probably the only one on the planet who hasn't. I'll get around to it one of these days. But I seldom go far so I think it would probably take me as long to set the thing up as to get there anyway. But, yes, good idea, I'll put it on my Christmas list."

He arrived at the house promptly at 6.30 as promised. "No trouble finding me then?" Karis was ready, waiting for him with a light-weight dark cream jacket on over a thin black wool dress with a high neckline with black patent sling-back shoes and a clutch bag. Spring was waiting in the wings but had not yet arrived and the evenings were still chilly enough to require an extra layer for warmth.

"You look very nice," he said, turning and leading her to his car. He opened the passenger door and she sat down and buckled the seat belt, not altogether sure whether she wanted to be where she was, but it was too late to have a change of mind so she had better try and relax and enjoy the evening and whatever it had in store for her.

In fact, the evening was a great success and Karis thoroughly enjoyed it. Bill introduced her to his sister, Fiona, and her husband, Jack, when they met in the foyer. Fiona looked a lot like Bill with softly waving light brown hair and brown eyes that registered that she was pleased to meet her. Karis immediately warmed to her.

The small theatre was already full of people when they climbed the stairs to the bar and although Karis sensed Fiona and Jack's interest in her, they were obviously feeling their own nervousness on behalf of their son, wondering how the play would go and be received by the audience. And it was such a crush and so noisy anyway, it was impossible to have a proper conversation with them. The four of them tried to make small talk while drinking their gin and tonics but gave up as it was just impossible to hear what anyone was saying.

The theatre was full to capacity with an air of cheerful anticipation and it didn't take long after curtain up to realise that the play was going to be a success. Karis turned to Bill and smiled, settled further into her seat and prepared to enjoy the rest of the evening.

"Would you like to come in for a coffee?" she asked when they arrived back at her house, not sure whether he would accept or not. And not knowing, either, whether she wanted him to or not.

"Thanks. Yes. That would be lovely," he said, switching off the engine and following her into the house. "I could do with some liquid refreshment and it'll finish the evening off very nicely."

"It won't take a minute. I hope you have no objection to having one of those filter coffee things which you just pour hot water on. I'm afraid I've grown quite lazy since I've been on my own and I look for the easy option regarding absolutely everything." Karis switched on the kettle and opened the biscuit tin. "And I am distinctly unimaginative when buying biscuits – I like Hob Nobs so that's what I buy. Sorry." She handed the tin to Bill to put some on a plate.

"Don't apologise. They are both fine by me. And since I, too, live alone, I go along completely with your logic. There is nothing wrong in feeding your own needs."

Bill stood up to take the tray of coffee and biscuits from Karis and put it on the coffee table.

"So you are not married then? I wasn't sure, since there has been no mention of a wife. No girlfriend either? I don't mean to be nosy but," she laughed, "I would like to know, purely for academic reasons you understand. And since you are an attractive man, I imagine that you must have had girlfriends at the very least, at some time or another."

"No gossip in the office then? I thought someone might have mentioned my marital state by now." He smiled at her. "Anyway, just to set the record straight, I was married but am now divorced. We didn't have children. I met Bella when we were both at university. We were besotted with each other and – you know the format I'm sure – couldn't possibly live without being in each other's pocket. Got married in a rush, against our parents' best advice – what did they know? - and then realised in a very short space of time and in the recognised format that our parents were right after all and we had made a terrible mistake. I admit I was not easy to live with, still trying to pass exams and not being the attentive 'new man' that Bella was looking for. Untidy, uncaring and sexually demanding, typical student I guess, and that was after we had been married for a couple of years! And from my point of view, she was pretty useless as well - couldn't cook, didn't do any housework, had never seen an iron so didn't know what it was for. We were really just a couple of kids playing at being grown-ups."

Karis smiled at him "As you say, it does all sound fairly familiar. It was pretty much the same for Jonathan and me, except we lasted a lot longer. At first, we just played at being married but the difference was that we got better at it and then it became unthinkable that we would ever be apart. We finished each other's sentences and could read each other's thoughts and were so comfortable with each other that I guess it finally worked against us. Too much taken for granted by both of us. But we did have children and both of them, Jamie and Joanne, are completely fed up with us both for having the temerity to split up without consulting them! They also expect us to get together again fairly soon and, initially, that's what I thought would happen too. Now

I'm not so sure." Karis paused and sipped her coffee, savouring the flavour. "We've both moved on, made new lives for ourselves and I think we may well be getting to the stage where there is no going back." Karis stopped talking and stared into the middle distance, cross with herself for revealing more than she had intended to. She had been surprised by Bill's candid confession about his own circumstances and had responded in kind without too much thought.

Recovering her composure, Karis continued. "Enough of all that. I thought the play tonight was brilliant. Please pass on my congratulations to your nephew when you next see him. He will be very thrilled with his first night and there is no reason why the play shouldn't get rave reviews in the press tomorrow, which will help to keep the theatre filled for the rest of the run. And thank you for thinking of me and giving me a thoroughly enjoyable night out. I am very grateful to you, Bill. It's been lovely."

"My pleasure, Karis. I'm glad you enjoyed it and, don't forget, you were getting me out of my sister's bad books so I am grateful to you for agreeing to come with me. Now I'd better get myself off home and leave you in peace. I've a visit to St Agnes's Hospital tomorrow morning anyway, so I need to be on the ball for that."

Bill stood up and made his way to the door. "You've got a delightful home, Karis, and the coffee and biscuits were just right." He bent his head and kissed her lightly on the cheek, his hand on her arm. "Thank you for coming with me this evening. Goodnight and I'll see you on Monday."

Karis sat mulling over the evening after Bill had gone, happy that it had been so enjoyable and that there had been no awkwardness between them and that meeting his sister and her husband had been pleasant and relaxed; perhaps she would meet them again. And then, quite suddenly, she felt very tired as she relaxed and, strangely happy. It was a good feeling.

Chapter 21

The following Thursday Karis was scheduled to visit The Pheasants to start work on Oliver's book collection. Now that Kate had become more friendly towards her, she found her fortnightly visits, usually lasting approximately three to four hours, very absorbing and enjoyable and she looked forward to going. The LP and CD collection had been sorted and Kate and her daughters would, by now, have decided which they were going to keep and which would either be sold or given to charity shops.

The book collection would be altogether more interesting and she couldn't wait to get started.

As usual, on her visits, Kate would have coffee either ready or almost ready for her arrival and they usually sat and chatted together for a while before Karis started work, either about family or current affairs or something they could share a laugh about. If Kate had noticed that Karis had been more preoccupied than usual on her last few visits, she didn't mention it and Karis had decided that she wouldn't say anything to Kate about Jonathan leaving her.

The truth was that she was still upset and raw about her current circumstances, feeling that somehow she was to blame; she was reluctant to acknowledge to herself that Oliver's legacy was in any way the cause of their problems, even though she thought it was more than likely that it was. Instead of giving them a reason for celebration at their good fortune, it had created just the opposite, causing suspicion and distrust between them, at least after the initial excitement when they first heard the news.

After coffee, Kate went with Karis into the study where she usually worked. One entire wall and half of another were filled with books of all sizes and descriptions, including atlases, dictionaries and reference manuals, tidily placed on shelves but in no real order. A set of wooden steps was propped against another wall and they would certainly be needed in order to get to the top shelves.

"Perhaps I'd better help you get the topmost books down, Karis," Kate said, "as they are too high for you to go up on your own without someone to hand them down to. The top two shelves anyway. What do you think?"

Karis agreed that that would be helpful and the two of them spent the next half an hour or so going up and down the steps, retrieving and then putting the books on the large oak desk that Oliver had used and which had been cleared completely, ready for Karis to start work. The desk was soon completely covered.

"Thanks, Kate. I think that is more than enough for me to be going on with today. But at least I can make a start."

It was obvious that the main bulk of Oliver's collection was to do with wars and conflict, going back over a couple of centuries, contrasting with his love of birds and wild flowers. He also had quite a few on American history and several British classics, including a complete set of Charles Dickens, so an eclectic mix.

Karis briefly wondered what she had let herself in for, becoming almost overwhelmed by the size of the job that was facing her. However, there was no hurry; Kate had intimated that Karis could take as long as she liked, saying how much she looked forward to seeing her on her fortnightly visits which took away some of the pressure she may have felt to finish the job as soon as possible. And Karis admitted to herself that she enjoyed visiting The Pheasants too as it took her into another world so completely different from the one she was usually involved with and was, therefore, stimulating and like taking a tonic.

She worked steadily for a while, putting the various books into piles and wishing that she had a bit more experience to make a better job of what she was doing. There were a huge number of factual books on both the Great War and World War II about the Army, the Navy and the RAF as well as autobiographies, biographies and books on strategy.

And then she came across *The Cruel Sea* – the book that she and Oliver had discussed at length and which both of them enjoyed reading very much. She picked it up, still in its paper cover and flicked through the pages stopping to read the odd paragraph or two as she did so. A folded sheet of paper fell out on to the floor and Karis bent to retrieve it, unfolding it as she picked it up. On one of the inside folded sides there was a drawing in pencil of a box which looked like a treasure trove trunk with the lid slightly open and falling out of one end was what looked like a string of pearls. The word 'Secret' was written on the front of the box.

Karis opened up the sheet of paper and saw that it had a few words of Oliver's handwriting on it. It read:

My Love.

Followed by Shakespeare's 18th Sonnet written out in full.

Karis sat, quite still with the piece of paper in her hand, lost in thought. It had obviously been written by Oliver – when? And why? This piece of paper, strictly speaking, was now Kate's property but should she draw her attention to it? Karis wondered whether Kate would

173

have seen it and then thought that she probably hadn't. She wondered whether she should show Kate or whether she should, at least for the time being, leave it where it came from. Karis thought that she could work out what Oliver had been trying to say but she wasn't sure. Had he written it at a time of stress or elation or what? She needed to think things through so, to give herself time, she put the folded paper back inside *The Cruel Sea*, and then placed it on the war novels pile and, abstractedly, picked up another book.

But try as she might, she found herself unable to concentrate on what she was supposed to be doing. Books were picked up from one pile and put down in another. She decided that it was time to plug in the laptop and get started on that but even then found her thoughts straying. For goodness sake, get a grip, she told herself and pay attention to what you are doing.

At last, it was time to go home. "I'm afraid I haven't made much of an impression on these books today, Kate. I'm sorry. Is it OK if I leave them where they are until I come again? They look a bit untidy all over the place, but maybe if you keep the door shut it won't be too much of a problem for you."

"It's no problem at all Karis. I'm not expecting visitors, except maybe Sara on Sunday, so they can stay where they are. I do hope I haven't put too much of a burden on you: I wouldn't want to do that and, as I've said, there is no hurry for you to finish the cataloguing. And thank you, as always, for coming anyway."

Karis slipped the car into gear and drove off, waving goodbye to Kate as she did so. It was good to think that Kate was getting her life back together again and she was far less likely to suddenly dissolve into tears these days. But what would she think of Oliver's note? Karis thought about it and decided that she would give it some consideration over the next couple of weeks as a decision would have to be made whether she should hand it over to Kate or not.

The telephone was ringing as Karis opened the front door. She ran to it and picked it up.

"Hi Mum. I was just about to give up on you. I thought you had Thursdays off work?"

"Hello Jamie. Yes, I do. But I am helping Kate Melrose out with some cataloguing of Oliver's books and pictures and music collection and I go over to The Pheasants every other Thursday morning to do just that. Actually, it makes a nice change from my usual ordinary run-of-the-mill work and I'm quite enjoying it. Hearing from you is an unexpected pleasure though – what do you want?" She laughed as she always teased him that he only called her when he wanted something.

Jamie laughed too. "You'll be pleased to hear I don't want anything! Or rather, I do in a way. I wanted to know if you'd be in on Saturday. I'm coming down to meet up with Tom White and I wondered whether you would have a bed for me for the night and then, maybe, I could take you and Dad out for lunch on Sunday?" Tom was an old school mate of Jamie's and they had kept in touch after going their separate ways after leaving school.

"Yes, of course you can stay the night. Not so sure about Sunday lunch though. I haven't seen your dad for a few weeks and when I did, I got the impression that he was pretty busy at weekends. Would you like to ring him and ask and then ring back and let me know? I think it might be better if you ring him yourself and ask."

"OK. I'll give him a call this evening and then ring you back when I know what's what. You won't be out will you, only I heard from Joanne that you had been out on a date recently?"

Did his tone sound a little disapproving? It was also questioning. Karis smiled to herself. What was it about children not liking their parents doing things which they considered normal for themselves but for some reason, not for them? "No. I won't be out. And I'll tell you all about that when I see you. 'Bye Jamie." And she put the phone down.

She kicked her shoes off, picked them up and then ran up the stairs to change her clothes. She'd decided that she would spend a couple of hours pottering in the garden; it was not as if it was neglected or needed much doing to it but it was a therapeutic need in her to commune with nature and the garden would appreciate the attention anyway.

Briefly, she thought about Jamie and his unexpected request for a bed for the night. There was no problem there and it would be good to see him and, also, she was pleased that Jamie had kept in touch with Tom as she thoroughly approved of their friendship; always had. They had been very close friends when they were teenagers and did their growing up together, both of them treating all the challenges that came their way, whether it was playing for the rugby team or strumming their guitars, loudly, with a huge sense of fun and with more enthusiasm than talent and somehow getting away with it. She hoped that Tom would come to the house before they went out so she could see him and see for herself how his life was working out and, with some subtle questions, find out whether he was a confirmed bachelor like Jamie. Somehow, she thought not.

Joanne, as expected, had telephoned Jamie soon after she and Jonathan had broken the news to her that they were separating, but apart from telling them that she had done so, she gave no indication what Jamie had said or whether he had expressed any opinion about their situation. Karis wondered whether he would want to talk about it while he was with her over the weekend, or while Jonathan was with them – always assuming that Jonathan would join them for lunch on Sunday – and she was not at all sure that she wanted to talk about it anymore: they had said just about everything that could be said, although she conceded that it was only right that Jamie should be put fully in the picture regarding their current situation.

Karis tugged at a milkweed that was reluctant to be removed from its nice warm spot just by the base of a clematis; it obviously had a root that was about a foot deep in the soil. Not one to give up easily, she eventually pulled it up feeling a small sense of victory on her achievement while telling herself that it was pathetic to feel that way over a weed. As always, after an hour or so of wondering where all the weeds had come from after such a short time and allowing her mind to go into freefall and feeling once more at peace with her world, she went into the kitchen to make a cup of tea, thinking she was glad she didn't have a lawn to look after.

Would Jonathan accept Jamie's invitation? Karis thought about it. He probably would, as he loved his son dearly and hadn't seen him for some while, and even though Karis would be there, she expected that he wouldn't mind that too much if he had a chance to chat with his son.

She and Jonathan rarely saw each other these days and when they did, Jonathan appeared to be perfectly happy with his new life. They occasionally spoke to each other on the telephone but no news of any significance had been forthcoming from him, the exception being to tell her that he was now working full-time and that he was coping very well with his extended hours. Obviously, he said, this makes paying all the bills so much easier, even leaving a bit left over so that he could pursue his new hobby of learning to play golf, which Karis thought very selfish; never once since leaving her had he enquired about her welfare or how she was coping with paying all her bills on the house, presumably making the assumption that everything was OK and that she was managing all right without him. He had made no mention of looking for somewhere to buy so Karis thought it probable that he was happy enough in the flat and that that idea had been put on hold for the time being. Maybe he would be more forthcoming about his plans for the future when he spoke with Jamie.

Karis ran herself a hot bath, pouring what was left of some rather exotic smelling bath oil she had been given at Christmas into the water and then lowered herself in for a nice long wallow. It had been quite an eventful day and it was rather a nice way to switch off from the stresses and strains and relax.

Jamie rang again as she was finishing supper. "Dad says he'd love to meet for lunch. OK for him to call round about 12 on Sunday morning? And, Mum, could you book a table for us please? I thought the Golden Lion at Holbrook – that always used to be very good so I'm hoping it still is and it'll save you having to cook. Lovely! Thanks. I'll be with you about 4ish then on Saturday afternoon. There are some things I need to do on Saturday morning. Love you." And he rang off.

Karis put the phone down. Jamie was always in a hurry, talking in short staccato bursts. He'd always been like that, even as a very small boy, wanting to know how everything worked, wanting to physically do things that were beyond his ability and his understanding, barely still during the day and falling asleep the moment his head touched the pillow; then waking refreshed, full of life and fun and ready to tackle whatever lay in store for him the next day. He had been the easiest of boys to look after, apart from trying to answer all his questions about absolutely everything and his love and loyalty were never in doubt, his undoubted affection for his parents and his sister being extended to and embracing his many friends.

Chapter 22

Jamie had his nose in the Sunday paper's sports section when Jonathan drove up in his car on Sunday morning. He was quiet and subdued after his night out with Tom (Karis assumed from over-indulgence) but, at breakfast, he had told Karis that Tom was getting married and he had asked Jamie if he would be his best man, to which Jamie had said yes, of course, he would be absolutely delighted.

Jamie had arrived on Saturday afternoon as planned and had clearly been very happy to see his mother, enveloping her in a bear hug and presenting her with a huge bunch of flowers.

"Lovely to see you, darling," Karis said, "and you're looking a picture of health and beauty!" They both laughed, straight away back into their old mother/son relationship as if he had never been away. "And the flowers are beautiful. Thank you."

Jamie had told her all about his current workload - heavy - and some amusing anecdotes about his colleagues and friends while they had tea and toasted crumpets. "Great, Mum. Don't remember the last time I had crumpets for tea," he had said, tucking in as if he hadn't eaten for days. He'd always had a healthy appetite and had never been a problem to feed.

Karis listened, delighted to have his company and to hear all about his current lifestyle, but there was no mention of any particular girlfriend and she wasn't about to ask him. He'd no doubt tell her when there was something to tell.

"What's the reason for seeing Tom?" she asked, more of a continuation of the conversation than curiosity.

"Not really sure, Mum. But I think it may be because he's met some girl and is thinking about getting married. Just a guess though."

Tom had called round to pick Jamie up at around 7.30 that evening, still looking amazingly boyish with his shock of brown hair, cut fashionably in such a way as to look as if he'd been pulled through a hedge backwards, his face wreathed in smiles. "Great to see you, Mrs Fielden. You are looking marvellous, as always."

"You still have the knack of saying the right thing, Tom. We could do with more like you," and she gave him a hug. "Thank you. And you're not looking so bad yourself either. I hope you are keeping well – although, looking at you, I'd say you were in the best of health!"

And then Jamie and Tom, grinning like a pair of Cheshire cats, had left Karis to her solitary evening and departed for their night out together like a couple of schoolboys, laughing and joking together. She had heard Jamie come in, fairly late, obviously trying to be very quiet and not quite achieving it, and had then fallen asleep; her old habit of not being able to sleep while either Jamie or Joanne or, come to think about it, Jonathan, was still out continuing as it had before when the three of them were still all living at home.

"Hi! Dad. Great to see you," Jamie greeted Jonathan as he opened the door to him, the men shaking hands. "I'm glad that you were able to make it today. Mum has booked us in at the Golden Lion at Holbrook for one o'clock and I'm looking forward to some roast beef. How about you? Is it still your favourite?"

"Yes it is. Nothing quite like it for a Sunday lunch and I am looking forward to it, especially as you are picking up the bill." Then turning to Karis, he said, "Hello, Karis. How are you?" and kissed her lightly on the cheek, smiling briefly as he did so but avoiding eye contact with her and making no comment on her new haircut. "If we go now, then, we can have a drink before lunch. Are you driving, Jamie, or am I?"

The Golden Lion was busy, full of people eagerly looking forward to a traditional Sunday roast and the noise levels were fairly high. There were flag stones on the floor of the pub which had been there for a couple of centuries ever since the pub had been built and the furniture was mostly dark oak, with hunting prints and horse brasses on the walls and the curtains and rugs were a mixture of deep crimson and dark green. It was warm, cosy and welcoming and the staff attentive, efficient and pleasant.

They were shown to a table in a window alcove which took them away from the main hub-hub of noise which Karis was pleased about as it would give them a better chance to have a conversation in spite of the noise in the main dining area. After giving the menu a cursory look, both Jamie and Jonathan opted for the roast beef, as expected, but Karis took a little longer making her decision, finally deciding to have the roast lamb. She and Jonathan had a gin and tonic and Jamie a pint of beer while waiting for the food to be served.

"So how's the job going then, Jamie? We don't hear much from you these days. Is everything working out OK for you?" Jonathan was looking expectantly at his son as he spoke.

"Yes, thanks, Dad. It's going really well. I work with a bunch of fairly dynamic people who are very talented, full of enthusiasm and brilliant ideas and energy and somehow it pulls me along trying to keep up with it all. The first couple of years I wondered whether

I would be able to deal with all the demands on my energy levels, not to mention my brain, but I guess, like everything else, you get used to it and the more familiar everything becomes the better you are able to cope. I just love the buzz of the place and I've even been given my own accounts now so I think that maybe I am just about accepted and can be considered part of the set up. But that's enough about me." He paused, looked at each of them in turn and then continued, "But I want to talk about you two. What on earth is going on? I couldn't believe it when Joanne telephoned me and said that you were going to separate. Why, for God's sake? You've been together for years and years. You've always been so happy and appeared to be so right for each other so what is different now? I look at you both and you look as you always have done, pretty normal and together. I just can't imagine why you've both taken such an odd decision and I'd appreciate hearing an explanation as I don't understand what is going on and I'd like it to be plausible 'cos for the life of me, I can't think of one." Jamie's voice had risen slightly as he had delivered his speech which he had obviously thought about beforehand, his face serious and showing both concern and exasperation at the misbehaviour of his parents.

Both Karis and Jonathan were taken aback by Jamie's words. Good Lord! thought Karis. Where on earth did that come from? Neither of them had expected a full-on tirade from their son. They were supposed to be out for a quiet family lunch but things had taken a slightly different direction from the way they had expected.

Just then, their food arrived which gave them both time to get their thoughts together as it was put on the table. I guess we should have anticipated Jamie's concern, Karis thought, but he hadn't given any indication at all that he was in the least bit bothered about them until now. And yet, surely as their elder child he had a right to have his say and to voice his opinion, even though it would make little difference to his own life.

The food was good, hot and tasty and all three ate steadily for a little while, each lost in their own, very different, thoughts.

Jamie particularly enjoyed his meal; it was what Sundays always used to be about. His London lifestyle was so different now and he wouldn't want to change it, not yet anyway, but it was great to sample some good old traditional food again.

Karis ate slowly, her enjoyment tempered by her thoughts on the explanation that Jamie was expecting them to give him. What was she going to say? Even more important, what was Jonathan going to say? And since he was the one who had left her, surely it was up to him to explain their situation. The silence between them continued until Jonathan said that he thought that it would be a good idea to continue their conversation when they got back home, Karis and Jamie both nodding their agreement.

"Jamie, darling, that was a lovely lunch and a real treat for us, thank you. I suggest that we have coffee when we get home and we can then chat at the same time. OK?" Karis wasn't expecting dissent and none was offered.

Jamie paid the bill and then the three of them piled into Jamie's car and he drove back to Karis's house, still in silence until Karis asked Jamie what time he would be leaving to drive back to London.

"I'd like to leave around four. Traffic always builds up soon after that with people going back after weekends away and I'd like to miss the worst of it if possible."

Karis went straight into the kitchen and brewed the coffee, making it stronger than she usually would. Why did I do that, she wondered. She also put a fruit cake on the tray before taking it into the sitting room; none of them had wanted pudding after lunch and she thought that both Jamie and Jonathan would like a slice, particularly Jamie.

"So," Jamie began, sipping his coffee, "I'm still waiting for an explanation. You two have upset my world and I'd like to know why. With everything else going on at work at least I thought I could count on you two maintaining the status quo at home."

Jonathan cleared his throat. "It's all very well you expecting that everything should stay the same, Jamie, but life is not like that. Nothing stays the same forever. As I said to Joanne, people change as they grow up and they go on changing through the various stages of their lives. It's not that Mum and I don't still care for each other, it's just that we've grown apart and we now want to do different things and we thought that we should get on and do those different things while we are still able. And it seems to be working very well; at least it is as far as I am concerned." He glanced at Karis who was staring at him in disbelief. Had he talked himself into believing all the rubbish he was talking, including her in his conclusions when, as far as she could remember, they applied only to him.

He went on, "This new job I've got has given me my confidence back. I'm learning how to play golf and I've joined the company sports club and I feel like a new man and much fitter and younger than I have for years."

For heaven's sake! Karis was exasperated beyond reason. Jonathan made himself sound like any other frustrated middle-aged man who suddenly found himself bored with his wife and wanted to spice his life up and was searching around for possible reasons why he could, and should, leave the marital home.

"Why don't you tell him the real reason why you left me?" Karis asked, looking directly at Jonathan who found it impossible to meet her eyes. "Your father thinks I had an affair, Jamie, years ago, but an affair nevertheless. And that was compounded by the fact that I was left a sum of money by my 'lover' which, in his mind, condemned me. I never wanted your dad to leave, I still love him as much as I did when we were first married but I'm not going to try and hold on to a man who doesn't want to be with me."

Jamie was looking shocked at this revelation. "God, Mum. I don't know what to say." Jonathan appeared not to have heard and was giving the carpet his full attention

"It's often a good idea to say nothing, Jamie. It would save a lot of trouble if people kept their mouths shut more often. Think things by all means, but say nothing." She felt sick and sad. Where was this going? And what was the point?

"Would you like some more coffee, either of you? There's plenty in the pot. And how about another piece of cake, Jamie?" Karis was trying desperately to behave as if everything was normal while swallowing hard to hide the lump in her throat. Why on earth am I bothering to behave as if everything is OK and still the same?

Jamie was obviously having second thoughts about his insistence on wanting to know what his parents were doing with their lives and he fervently wished he hadn't asked. It was, after all, up to them what they did. It was just that he desperately wanted them to be together so that they could all play at 'happy families' and he thought that he could help to make it better again. The older he got the more he realised that happiness often came at a price and was seldom a feeling that was felt equally between two people and neither did it come without a great deal of hard work and dedication.

They waved Jamie off at just before 4 o'clock, still crestfallen and looking very serious. "Thanks for having me, Mum. I was going to suggest you come up to town to see a show both of you, but that is probably not a good idea right now. Perhaps later on in the year." He kissed his mother and gave her a hug and then shook his father's hand. "I love you both. Take care of yourselves."

"I guess I'd better be going too,' Jonathan said as Jamie disappeared . "I told the boys I'd meet them for a game of snooker and a pint at the club this evening and I've one or two things to do before then. I guess it's just as well that Jamie and Joanne know the situation as it is. No point in trying to keep the truth from them and trying to gild the lily."

They were both thinking that it was likely that Jamie would call Joanne that evening to chat to her about his visit. Did children usually care very much what happened to their parents, particularly after they had grown-up and left home? Jonathan was sure they didn't but Karis was not convinced; she thought it possible that she would hear from Joanne again soon.

"Absolutely not! No point at all." Karis's voice was cold, her face set. She couldn't wait for him to be gone. "You mustn't keep your jobs and your friends waiting."

She had had enough of company for the weekend and was looking forward to some peace and quiet, a glass of wine and maybe some meaningless TV. And to hell with Jonathan and whatever he was going to do. She didn't care. She really, really didn't care!

From now on there would be no more overtures from her to try and get him to change his mind. He was obviously content to be on his own – if he was on his own – and as far as she was concerned, that was that! She, too, would get on with her life, in peace.

Chapter 23

Maybe it was the glass of wine, or two, that helped but Karis fell asleep that night almost as soon as her head touched the pillow. She had gone over the events of the last couple of days in her head during the evening, thinking how nice it had been to have Jamie home – that had been the good bit – and how completely un-nerving it had been to hear Jonathan tell Jamie how happy he was now that he had left her. Somewhere along the way she must have lost the plot, as she had always felt that she and Jonathan were as happy as any other couple or friends that they knew. She'd got on with her life assuming, taking for granted would be a better way of describing it she reminded herself, that everything was fine and getting better again after their traumas.

However, Jonathan had painted a picture where he had gone from being the villain of the peace, having squandered their nest egg and lost his job, to someone who had then been ill and needed her wholehearted attention. And then the wronged husband who was now enjoying a new lease of life with a new job on his own and, most important of all, it seemed, without her.

She tried to convince herself that it was all just part of life's rich tapestry and it was necessary to experience all the emotions to be able to appreciate what life was all about, but it all seemed so unfair and the prospect of spending the rest of her life alone and without Jonathan living with her, still filled her with dread.

She hadn't protested too much when Jonathan had said that he was going to leave her, as she had not thought that he meant it seriously and that after a time of being on his own, he would be back again, at least within a few months. But it was now more than six months and he appeared, genuinely, to be enjoying himself and gave no indication at all that he would ever come back to her. Well, if that was the case, she had better get on and start enjoying her life too – it was too short to waste it on regrets and what might or might not have been.

And yet the more she thought about it the more she realised that she was a one man girl and that one man had been Jonathan from the first time they had met and, she felt her eyes begin to fill with tears, it was Jonathan still. He had always said, with great tenderness, that he would love her forever but he had obviously forgotten because that was then and this was now and they were now worlds apart.

She had thought that he wouldn't look after himself properly but he had proved her wrong, appearing smartly dressed, always with a clean shirt and clean shaven and with his - still brown – hair nicely trimmed, although she noticed that there was a little more grey now in his sideburns. She told herself that she was glad that he was coping well on his own but she again asked the question that was in her head and refused to go away, is there another woman now with him?

Of course, spending time with Jamie and Jonathan had meant that she hadn't had a chance to ask Jonathan any personal questions but she was pretty sure that he was happy not to be alone with her anyway. Had he any regrets? Perhaps she would give him a ring during the week to see if he would come round for dinner one night; knowing how much he enjoyed his food, she could cook something that she knew he particularly liked and then maybe he would open up a bit. But then again, perhaps she wouldn't. She felt demoralised enough without piling more humiliation and agony on herself and hearing him say things that she didn't want to hear. No. She definitely wouldn't contact him.

I must get out more, she told herself. Maybe I could join a tennis club and meet some new people; I must do something other than work or I shall go mad.

But a good night's sleep worked wonders and when Karis woke up on Monday morning, feeling bright and refreshed, she put her troubles behind her feeling optimistic that things could, and would, get better.

And they did. Bill Matthews called her into his office on Tuesday morning and after enquiring how she was, asked her if she would do him a favour, another one, and go with him to a party that was being given by a friend and colleague of his on Saturday evening. It would be very informal, buffet food and drink and no pressure whatsoever – how about it?

Karis didn't hesitate –"Love to," she said smiling happily. "What time?"

"Party starts at eight. I'll pick you up at nine. We should be there at 9.30 by which time things should be in full swing. Wear your prettiest dress. Love your hair, by the way. It suits you and takes ten years off your age."

"Thanks. That's what the hairdresser said but then that's no surprise is it? He's hardly going to say it looks awful after he'd just spent a couple of hours transforming me. My husband didn't mention it at all when I saw him at the weekend. But my son liked it so some you win and some you lose." She smiled at him. "I shall look forward to Saturday. Meantime, I've a lot of work in my in-tray - don't you medics ever stop? – so, I had better get on with it. Thanks, Bill. You've made my day."

From then on, Karis and Bill usually went out together once or twice a week, either to the theatre, or to a pub for a meal and sometimes just for a walk and a drink in the country. Bill was very much the townie, having been born in a town centre where he was most comfortable surrounded by concrete, theatres, museums and art galleries, but he enjoyed listening to Karis explain the country code to him and he teased her when she told him the name of all the flowers they saw on their country walks saying that she was making them up as she went along. Their companionship was just that, company for each other; not once did Bill make any move or say anything to her that was in any way out of place or could be treated as anything other than friendly.

In fact, although Karis was extremely happy in Bill's company and it was never dull as they discussed and argued about everything under the sun, she did wonder whether perhaps she had lost her sex appeal or whether he was just not very interested in sex. Their evenings always ended with him giving her a peck on the cheek and once or twice Karis found herself wishing that he would put his arms around her and kiss her properly. If she thought about it at all and was honest with herself, she missed having love and intimacy in her life, although she wasn't at all sure how she would handle it if Bill did make a move on her. Was she ready for sex? She pondered the question and decided she didn't know. But since the question hadn't arisen anyway, as Bill didn't appear to be even remotely interested in her in that way, it didn't really matter.

Again, she thought about Jonathan. She hadn't seen him for quite a while now and there hadn't even been a phone call between them. Presumably everything was OK with him. And then it occurred to her that she had thought about him and hadn't felt the stomach churning that she usually felt, the hurt was obviously getting less. Perhaps she would give him a call at the weekend just to make sure he was OK and also test her own reactions to the sound of his voice. Perhaps, at last, she was getting over the pain of their separation or, if not that, at least getting used to it.

It was several weeks after Jamie had stayed that Karis had an excited text message from Joanne. 'Lee has asked me to marry him and I said yes. Isn't it marvellous? Lots of love, x'.

Karis felt elated and very happy with the news; how good to hear something that lifted the spirits and, knowing how much Joanne had been longing for Lee to pop the question, Karis texted a reply at once. 'Wonderful news, darling. Can't wait 2 hear all about it. Congrats to you both x x'.

Should she ring Jonathan or had Joanne texted her dad as well? She decided that she would ring him that evening as she had a real reason to do so now, and she assumed that Joanne would also have texted her brother.

"Jonathan Fielden," his voice sounded tired and disinterested. Just in time, Karis stopped herself from saying 'Hello darling' and substituted "Hello Jonathan," instead. "How are you? I'm not interrupting anything am I? You're not in the middle of dinner?"

"No, I've had supper already and am just about to make some coffee and read the paper. What are you calling about? Nothing too disastrous I hope." He was obviously hoping that she wasn't going to impart bad news.

"No, nothing disastrous at all; quite the reverse in fact. I've had a text from Joanne today saying that Lee has asked her to marry him. She sounded very excited and I wondered whether she had texted you as well?

Anyway, I thought you should know as soon as possible so that's why I'm ringing. She sounds very thrilled about it all and I expect she will be in touch again soon but I don't imagine that they plan to get married for some while yet anyway so, no need for us to panic."

"I guess it was fairly inevitable as they appeared to be so happy together. No I haven't heard from her but I suppose it's usual to contact Mum before Dad in this sort of situation, knowing how rapturous and unnecessary women get about weddings." His voice was showing a bit more interest but was still fairly lack-lustre. "I hope she's not planning on having a big 'do' as there still isn't a lot of money sloshing around, unless, of course, you've still got some of your ill-gotten gains handy." He laughed, and then realising that that was probably the wrong thing to say, said, "Sorry. I didn't mean to say that. It just sort of slipped out."

"That's a mean thing to say Jonathan, and you know very well that everything I have was put towards buying this house." Karis's voice showed her annoyance at his snide remark and his comment had caused her to lose some of her enthusiasm.

"In answer to your query, I've no idea what sort of wedding Joanne is planning but I doubt she's even thought about it in detail yet. One thing at a time, first the ring...and go on from there. But I don't imagine they plan to have the ceremony for quite some while yet anyway. With Lee's parents abroad at the moment - I'm not quite sure where they are - any planning that Joanne and Lee do will be long-range. I expect Joanne will be in touch again soon and maybe she'll be planning to visit to talk about things with us. Will you want to come over?"

"Yes. I guess so. Give me a ring when you hear from her," and he put the phone down.

Not even a goodbye, thanks for calling! How times had changed. It was like talking to a stranger, Karis thought as she replaced the receiver, not her long-time husband and soul-mate. Was he pleased? Did he care? And then as an after-thought, I hope he's not lapsing into depression again. He had sounded so weary which was a long way away from the man who had been so bright and full of confidence when Jamie had been down not so long ago.

Karis sent Joanne a text asking her to text or ring her father, telling her that she had told him the good news but suggesting that he would appreciate hearing directly from her as well.

With a cup of tea in her hand, Karis wandered out onto the patio to sit and have a think about things. The sun was still fairly high in the sky, giving off enough warmth to necessitate the sunshade to be erected over the patio table. Karis could smell the scent from the Gertrude Jekyll rose which was trained up the wall to the left and was sharing the space with a purple clematis she had inherited from the previous owners, together the plants producing a riot of colour. In fact, the garden was looking lovely and, as it always did, restored some peace and tranquillity into her mind as she thought about the happy prospect of a wedding in the family.

Yes, a wedding, in a year or so would be lovely. It would give them plenty of time to think about and to plan for; she just hoped that Joanne's expectations matched her own ideas and that she wasn't set on something wildly extravagant or outside the realms of reality. Meantime, there was no harm in her ringing a few local country hotels and getting their brochures so that she could start estimating suitability, not to mention costs.

Chapter 24

This will be my last visit to The Pheasants, Karis thought as she drove through the countryside. The CDs and LPs had all been dealt with and the books sorted and catalogued; the stored paintings had been mostly sold and Kate had promised that she would make her final choice of the paintings she was going to keep or give to the family before Karis's visit today. It had been a bigger job than either of them had anticipated when it was started but now that it was nearly finished, Karis realised that she had thoroughly enjoyed every minute of her job and would miss her fortnightly visits which had taken her out of her usual predictably humdrum existence.

Although she hadn't said so in as many words, Karis felt that Kate had been giving a lot more thought to selling The Pheasants and moving into somewhere smaller after all, so getting her job finished would be a kick-start to getting other things decided as well as it would be one less thing to worry about.

Kate had mentioned to Karis, recently, that she didn't think her housekeeper would want to go on staying with her for much longer as she was nearing retirement age herself and there was no way Kate would be able to stay on in the house on her own without help. Idly guessing at the possible value of the house, Karis thought it likely that with the money Kate got from the sale of The Pheasants she would be in a position to be able to buy a small flat in London and also, possibly a small cottage in the country as well. She could see how reluctant Kate would be to leave The Pheasants but it would probably be better to sell now rather than wait until it all became an impossible burden for her. It was not a problem I'd have any difficulty coping with, she thought wryly.

It was a lovely warm morning in early summer, the hedgerows and roadside banks full of cow parsley or Queen Anne's lace as her mother would have called it, red campion and ox-eyed daisies and, here and there, a wild purple or mauve orchid. The grass was long, lush and green and the air still with scarcely a breath of wind to stir the trees. Hopefully, it was leading up to a warm summer to come. Suddenly aware that she was dawdling, Karis looked into her rear mirror and realised that she had been paying too much attention to the scenery and not enough to getting on with getting to The Pheasants as there was quite a few cars following her; she had better stop meandering and dreaming and put her foot down.

As usual, Kate had coffee ready for her arrival. "Hello, Karis. Lovely day isn't it? Too nice to work though so I hope you can finish off what you've got to do and you can then enjoy the rest of the day. Sarah is here for a few days and she'd like to join us for lunch and to say hello before you leave."

Karis felt her stomach give a lurch. She hadn't seen Sarah since Oliver's funeral when their contact had been brief and polite but remembering what Kate had said that Sarah thought that there may have been something between Oliver and herself for him to have left her such a large legacy, she wasn't at all keen to see her now. Did she still think that? Or had Kate conveyed to her daughter what Karis had told her that it could only have been in appreciation of her work for him over a number of years that had prompted his generosity to her.

The sunny day that had been with her as she had driven to The Pheasants, suddenly became overcast, but there was nothing she could do but get on with what she had come for. She would tidy up all the loose ends and finish what she had to do and then leave as soon as possible; making the excuse that she had something else to do in the afternoon. She really didn't want to see Sarah.

"And I'd like to have a word too, Karis. I've been doing a lot of thinking and have made a few major decisions and also, I know that you are not bothered about being paid for what you have been doing for me but that wasn't our agreement and, although I've written you a small cheque, I would like you to chose a book and a painting for yourself from those that we are not keeping, as a momentum and as a small token of my thanks for all your hard work."

Kate's speech was unexpected and Karis was taken by surprise. She couldn't think what to say except "Thank you, Kate. That's very generous and kind of you. I'll get on now with what needs to be done to finish everything off. Thanks for the coffee."

Karis made some phone calls regarding the collection of the unwanted pictures and books and she also spoke to a book dealer with whom she had arranged the purchase of several specialist books; she finished filling in tables and columns listing all the paintings and signed off the lists of CDs and LPs so that Kate had a complete set of all the transactions that had been made and also of those that had been kept either by Kate or the family. It was quite a task and when Karis finally finished she was both tired and elated at the same time.

She had also chosen to keep *The Cruel Sea* and a small water colour of a wild flower meadow in spring which was absolutely charming, as her personal keepsakes from Oliver's collections, and she was delighted with both. She had just the right spot to hang the painting in her cottage and she would also enjoy reading *The Cruel Sea* again. It would also take care of the problem of what to do with Oliver's note she had found in the book. It could stay where it was.

"I do hope you'll stay and have some lunch with Sarah and me, Karis. Nothing very much, just some mushroom vol au vents, biscuits and cheese and fruit?" Kate had come quietly into the study. "I can see you've just about finished now. It's been a great achievement Karis and I'm grateful to you for sorting it all out for me." She handed Karis an envelope, "Just a small thank you from me to you for all your hard work. Now, how about that lunch and a glass of wine by way of celebration? You deserve it."

"Both sound good. Thanks, Kate." Karis decided that it would be churlish of her to refuse to have lunch, especially as she had been asked specifically to stay. "And thank you for the cheque. It's much appreciated."

The two women left the study and walked into the sitting room where Sarah was standing by the fireplace looking completely relaxed and immaculate in a pair of smartly tailored black trousers and long-line cardigan over a silk blouse, both in soft baby blue. Her pale blonde hair was in a French pleat and her makeup peach perfect, making Karis immediately feel that she should have spent a little more time on her own makeup that morning.

"Hello Karis," Sarah said, her voice cool but not unfriendly. "Mother says you've been working very hard sorting out all Dad's books and things. One gets used to seeing books and LPs and things around without really realising just how many there are but it's a job that needed to be done and Jane and I just wouldn't have had the time to do it or, I may add, the patience or the expertise. I think it is time for us all to have a drink in celebration of a job very well done."

She poured three glasses of sparkling white wine and then handed her mother a glass and then one to Karis, before raising her own and saying, "Happy memories of a dearly loved husband and father," which wasn't quite what Karis was expecting. She sipped her wine which was absolutely delicious and looked at Kate, half expecting that she would be tearful but she was smiling and calm.

"Mother has been making some major decisions, Karis. You tell Karis, Mother." Sarah sat down on the nearest chair and Kate and Karis followed suit.

"As you know, Karis," Kate began, "I've been mulling over in my mind whether I should stay but, much as I love the house, it is too much for me to look after on my own. And although it has lots of happy memories, it also constantly reminds me how lonely I am without Oliver so I am putting it up for sale. I shall look for a small flat in London so I am nearer Jane and my grandchildren and also Sarah, of course, and I shall hope, too, to buy a small cottage not too far from this village. I love the area and have several friends with whom I wish to keep in contact so, if all goes according to plan, I shall have the best of both worlds. What do you think, Karis?"

"I think that that sounds like a wonderful idea, Kate. The Pheasants is a beautiful house but it is essentially, a family home and it needs people in it to fill the rooms with music and laughter and family noise! I'm sure you'll have absolutely no problem selling it as there must be lots of people queuing up waiting for something like this to come on the market. In a way it reminds me of the house that Jonathan and I had when we were first married, although it is much bigger than that of course.

It had four bedrooms, high ceilings, a big central hall and landing, Victorian plumbing – updated but still temperamental – but essentially, a happy house." Karis smiled at the memory.

"I take it you don't live there any longer? Did you downsize?" Sarah asked.

"No. Well, yes, I suppose we did but that wasn't the main reason for leaving the house. Unfortunately, my husband lost a great deal of money, and his job, on a business venture which went wrong and we had to move out as we could no longer afford to pay the mortgage and the running expenses. And he then suffered a nervous breakdown. Both Jamie and Joanne had already left home so the two of us could easily manage in a smaller house. It was like going from the sublime to the ridiculous as the cottage I am now in is very small. However, it serves a purpose and is just about adequate for my needs."

"You say you are now in. Are you living there on your own? Has something happened to your husband?" Sarah and Kate were both looking questioningly at Karis.

During the months that Karis had been visiting Kate at The Pheasants she had not mentioned the fact that Jonathan had left her; she felt there hadn't been the need. She was there to do a job and help Kate and she hadn't considered it either relevant or necessary to tell her of Jonathan's decision to 'go it alone'.

After a quick thought, Karis decided to bite the bullet. "Jonathan left me at the end of last year. He has now got a new job, having recovered from his breakdown and is happily living by himself in a flat. We are both fine." Karis felt that that was all they needed to know. She smiled weakly and took another sip of her wine.

Both Kate and Sarah were looking stunned at the news. "I'm so sorry, Karis," said Kate, "I had no idea. I've been selfishly thinking about myself all this time and hadn't given your personal life a thought, as you'd given no indication at all that you were unhappy. Is there any chance you will get together again?"

"At the moment, I've no idea Kate. I'd like to think so, but I really don't know." Karis was feeling uncomfortable and wishing that the subject hadn't come up and she could also see that Sarah's mind had gone into overdrive. "This wine is delicious," she said, taking another sip and trying to change the subject.

"Perhaps Jonathan was upset about the money that Dad left you," Sarah said, putting her thoughts into words and thinking that maybe she had been right all along about the legacy. "I would have thought that most men would have questions to ask about an amount of money that large being left to their wife by another man." Her voice was quiet but questioning.

Kate was looking horrified and glaring at her daughter and Karis was momentarily lost for words. How bloody dare she? Sarah had at last voiced her disapproval to her face and, in doing so, had brought her suspicions out into the open without any thought for the affect it would have on Karis. How could she handle it without being rude? She looked at Kate who was now looking at her with sympathy but also with a question mark in her eyes, waiting for her answer.

"No. He wasn't. The fact that the money was left to me at a time when we were short of both money and luck was nothing more than fortuitous and Jonathan knew very well that it was in recognition of my hard work for Oliver over a number of years. Nothing else." Karis's voice was cold and sounded shrill to her own ears and she felt tears beginning to gather in her eyes.

Angrily, she blew her nose. "I'm sorry Kate. I'm probably tired and I don't want to talk about Jonathan any more except to say that we are still friends and we still get together as a family when either Jamie or Joanne visits."

Sarah had the good grace to look contrite, regretting that she had brought the legacy up. She topped up Karis's glass. "We may as well finish the bottle off with lunch. Speaking of which, I'm hungry. Shall we go and eat?" For all the world as if they had been discussing the shopping or the weather or something equally mundane, Karis thought! However, she was determined that she would not get involved in a show of bad manners and since it appeared that perhaps Sarah was having regrets about broaching the subject of the legacy, Karis decided that she was satisfied that she had made her point.

For the rest of the meal, Sarah was both amusing and attentive while the three of them ate and drank and, boosted by the wine and some delicious food, Karis felt herself gradually relaxing and regaining her composure.

There was still a slight atmosphere in the air, though, which wouldn't have been there if Sarah hadn't brought up the subject of the legacy but what had been said couldn't be unsaid. However, Karis thought that it was unlikely that Sarah would refer to the subject again.

Kate walked with Karis to her car when she was leaving to go home. "I'm sorry that Sarah said what she did about the money Karis. I didn't know she was going to do that otherwise I would have stopped her. Over the last few months I've got to know you very well and I know how hard you can work and I'd like you to know that I have absolutely no worries about your relationship with Oliver. He was very lucky to have you look after him at the office. I hope that we can meet for lunch now and again when I get my accommodation sorted out as

I've grown to value your friendship and I'd very much like us to remain friends. I'll keep in touch and let you know how I get on with my buying and selling exercise. I just hope it all works out OK."

"I'm sure it will, Kate. And I, too, enjoy our friendship and look forward to keeping in touch. Goodbye for now and take good care of yourself."

Chapter 25

It was on a damp, drizzly, Saturday morning in town when Karis was coming out of a coffee shop that she spotted Jonathan across the road, standing quite still and looking into the distance as if he was waiting for someone. She was just about to cross the road to speak to him when she saw a youngish woman with long, dark brown hair, wearing a smart tan jacket and cream trousers tucked into tan boots walk up to him and kiss him briefly on the lips. Karis paused, midway across the road unsure whether to continue and speak to him or pretend she hadn't seen him. He was smiling now, looking into the face of the woman for all the world as if nobody else existed in the world and Karis thought that as he probably hadn't seen her, she could walk the other way.

Just as she changed direction, she heard her name being called and she turned to see him looking directly at her and smiling broadly so she continued to walk towards him.

"Karis. I thought it was you. I'd like you to meet a friend of mine. This is Louise. She works in the Treasury Department at work and is a very clever girl. Louise, this is Karis, my wife." There was no embarrassment in his voice.

Karis found herself holding out her hand and looking into smiling brown eyes. There was no question mark there, just a friendly look so it was probable that Jonathan had told Louise about her. "Hello, Louise. How are you?" she said, uncertain what else she should say and surprising herself by not betraying her true feelings which were anything but calm.

"I'm fine, thank you, Karis. Jonathan has told me about you. What a pretty name Karis is. Your parents obviously had more imagination than mine. The trouble is, unless I am firm about being called Louise, people tend to shorten it to Lou! Enough said." She laughed easily, her face tranquil and pretty. Karis thought that she was likely to be in her mid thirties so Jonathan wasn't quite cradle snatching but she wasn't that much older than his daughter and, as they appeared to be very familiar with each other, she wondered just how long Louise had featured in his life.

"Are you doing some serious shopping Jonathan, or just having a morning in town?" And not waiting for his answer and turning to Louise, she said, "I'm on my way to meet one of my old girlfriends from the company I used to work for. It'll no doubt be a very noisy, gossipy hour or so, but I'm very much looking forward to it." Anticipating Jonathan's question she smiled, briefly at him, and said that everything was fine, there were no problems.

He looked relieved "Good. I hadn't heard from you for some time so I assumed everything was OK."

The cheek of the man! As if the only time he heard from her was when she needed help with something. As long as she didn't do anything to rock the boat or cause him a problem, he was happy. She gritted her teeth, smiled pleasantly at them both and said she'd better be going. "It's been nice to meet you Louise. Goodbye Jonathan," and she re-crossed the road and continued on her way to meet Helen.

"Guess what Helen?" Karis said as soon as she saw her, "I've just bumped into my husband with another woman - a young and pretty one." Karis could hardly wait to tell Helen of her meeting and blurted out her news before Helen had even had chance to sit down, still not sure how she really felt about seeing her husband with another woman.

"Oh dear! You'd better tell me all about it." Helen sat down after kissing Karis on both cheeks, picking up the menu as she did so. "I think I fancy something extravagant today. How about you, Karis? Go on. I recommend that you should spoil yourself. If you've had a shock you need some comfort food, not to mention a nice big glass of wine."

"I don't need much persuading, Helen. An ice-cold glass of Chablis to go with a prawn salad I think. What are you going to have?" Helen made her selection, Lobster thermidor, gave their orders to the waitress and then turned to Karis. "Go on, then. Tell me all about it. I'm dying to hear."

Since the time that Karis had bumped into Helen after she had been to the agency, they had met several times, having mutually enjoyed their reunion very much. They found that between them they had much in common and Karis enjoyed the benefit of having someone who was not family to share her feelings and confidences with and to know that there would be no hasty judgement passed, just good unbiased advice. At the same time, she very much appreciated Helen's dry and, sometimes, outrageous sense of humour, which often sent her into peals of laughter while at the same time wondering how Helen had the nerve to say the things that she did. "It doesn't matter who it is, Karis, or what position they attain or do not attain in life, they are only human beings which means they are just like you and me and should be treated as such, always with courtesy and good manners, sometimes with kindness but absolutely no falling over backwards to please – or appease!"

207

"The thing is, Helen, I've had this feeling for some time that Jonathan maybe had another woman in his life," Karis began. "On the few occasions when I've seen him since he left me, he has always looked well turned out, not something he could manage without a great deal of encouragement when he lived with me, and it has been more what he hasn't said than what he has that made me think that. Do you know what I mean? Anyway, I was in the High Street when I saw him, obviously waiting for someone and then there she was, this lovely long-legged brunette, not quite the age of his daughter but certainly about fifteen years younger than he is. I thought he hadn't seen me but as I was walking away, trying to avoid him seeing me, he called to me which made it impossible for me to pretend I hadn't seen them and then he introduced me to Louise. He described her as a very clever girl from Treasury, which means she's good with money I guess, which is likely to be only the half of it!"

Their wine was put on the table and both Karis and Helen sipped from their glass. "Go on then, Karis. Tell me what happened then."

"Nothing much, really. She appeared friendly and outgoing and said that Jonathan had told her about me and that was about that. I managed to stop myself from behaving like a complete idiot by revealing my true thoughts, said I was meeting you so waved them goodbye and left them to it. Why is it that I can never think of a killer put-down when I need one?"

"Hmm. So how do you feel about it? Did you want to scratch her eyes out and tell her to leave your man alone? Or did you rise above it all and give them the impression that it didn't matter at all and that you had better things to do? I do hope it was the latter." Helen smiled at Karis and took another sip of her wine.

"To be honest, Helen, I don't know how or what I feel. Surprise at seeing them together maybe, but I've had this feeling for some time now that he had met another woman so it wasn't altogether unexpected to see them together. But, when you've been with a man for a very long time, you tend to think of them as your property so I have to admit that I did, briefly, contemplate scratching her eyes out or causing her harm! However, my self-control took over from my basic instincts and I just left them to it." Karis was surprised how calm she felt.

She continued. "And I can't act the innocent, can I? I've been going out with Bill Matthews for several months now and although we are genuinely just good friends, to all intents and purposes, we are a couple and we could have bumped into Jonathan at any time when we've been out for dinner or for a drink in a pub and, if we had, what would he have thought?"

"Probably the same as you I would think. That looks good." Helen smiled at the waitress as the food they had ordered was put on the table and the two women started to eat

"This is delicious," Karis said, mouth full of food. "How's yours and what have you got to tell me?"

"Ditto. I seem to enjoy everything I have when I am eating out. It must, perhaps, be something to do with not having had to get it in the first place. I don't know about your Karis, but I admit to getting lazier with each passing year. How I am going to manage when I am in my dotage, alone and penniless, heaven only knows! Shall just have to hope that never happens." She continued happily eating for a minute or two before looking up and smiling at Karis.

"Guess who I met the other evening? No. You'll never guess so I'll tell you. Drew Harman. You remember him, Karis, don't you? He was the finance director's right hand man and a bit of a dish. He is still a gorgeous looking bloke with the most startling blue eyes – just like Paul Newman - who systematically worked his amorous way through most of the women in the department and got away with it because he was so charming and sweet to them all. Plus, he was also very good at his job and the fact that he wasn't married probably helped! Unfortunately, he never tried it on with me." Karis wasn't sure whether Helen meant that or not.

"Yes. Of course I remember him. How could I not? Even though I was sort of cut off from the rest of the work force and in my own office, I still managed to keep up with some of the extra-work activities and gossip, courtesy of the personnel director's secretary who kept me reasonably well informed about the 'extra' social activities that went on between people. But, frankly, I was glad I was out of all that. Anyway, where did you meet him?"

"At the Jazz Club that's attached to the Fox and Hounds. Do you know it? Nice place where you can dance about a bit and make a fool of yourself if you feel like it with no one passing any comment – all very relaxed. He was there with another man who I didn't recognise. Anyway, we chatted a bit and he told me that he is now working as financial manager for a company that makes precision instruments, they are very busy and he is happy there. We talked about a few of the old team and he asked me if I had heard that Oliver had died; apparently, he thought very highly of him and he said that his present boss could do with some of Oliver's man management. He's still unmarried but said that was down to bad luck on his part and that he was still looking. I don't know whether he was serious or not but he was nice to chat to, even though he didn't ask me out at the time, although I live in hope as he asked for my mobile number!"

"Could be better luck next time then Helen. Are you getting fed up with being on your own?"

"Not really. Well, not all the time anyway but if the right man came along I may be persuaded to give it a go. How about you? Are you and this nice Bill Matthews going to get closer or are you still hoping that Jon's mid-life crisis will be over soon and he'll be back to beg you to have him back?"

"It doesn't much look like that is likely to happen at the moment does it? And I honestly don't know what I want. I sometimes feel like a lovesick adolescent who must have love and companionship and attention and then I think, no I don't, I enjoy being by myself. And do I want Jonathan back again - he is, after all, the father of my children and the man with whom I have spent most of my life, or do I want someone new with whom I would have to go through the process of getting to know what his likes and dislikes are, sharing a bathroom and a bedroom..." her voice trailed off. Then she grinned at Helen. "No! No! Far too much trouble. I'll stay the way I am, thank you. Although, I must admit I miss having someone there to share things with - a newspaper headline, a political gaff, some new clothes..." again her voice stopped. "And there's nothing like a good argument to lead on to good sex is there? Come to think about it, Helen, we two are a bit sad aren't we?"

Helen grinned at her. "Absolutely not! I love my life – I'm thinking of getting a dog!" and they both collapsed with laughter.

After getting the Sunday paper from the local shop next morning, skimming through it while drinking her coffee,

Karis thought she would take advantage of yesterday's soft rain and do some tidying up in the garden and also move an old hydrangea which had grown too big for the spot it was in against the back wall of the patio. She collected her fork and spade from the lean-to container where she kept her gardening things, together with her gardening gloves and started to put the fork in the earth, which was nicely soft, all round the plant to loosen it. This shouldn't be too difficult she told herself, pushing the fork deeper into the earth and straining with her arms and shoulders to lift the plant. It was very heavy and was much more difficult than she had anticipated, the roots going deep into the ground. After several attempts she realised that she had to stand at right angles to the plant to get behind it which made it even more difficult to lift the fork. Eventually, she felt the roots begin to give and, as she did so, she felt a pull in her right shoulder and a very sharp pain.

Gathering all her strength, she lifted the fork with the hydrangea on it and straining under the weight, she walked to the other side of the patio and put it down into a hole she had already prepared. The border was broader here, which would give the plant more room to spread. Her shoulder felt like it was on fire but, determined to finish the job and working mostly with her left arm she covered the roots of the plant and then feeling dizzy with the pain, put the tools away and went into the house.

She sat for several minutes recovering from her exertions and wondering what she was going to do. Had she dislocated her shoulder? She thought not but she had done something and that something was very painful and moving it, at least for the moment, wasn't an option. She decided to make herself a cup of tea and she would then decide after she'd had it what she should do and in all probability, by then, the shoulder would be OK again.

It wasn't. Her whole shoulder was screaming with pain and any movement was agony. Instinctively, she thought of Jonathan; he'd know what to do. With great difficulty and holding her arm close to her body in an effort to keep it still, she managed to tap in Jon's number. There was no answer and no answer phone either. Now what? Text him. Karis retrieved her mobile from her handbag and sent a brief text- Have hurt my shoulder can you please come round?

Two hours later and Karis had not had a reply. Obviously he was out somewhere with his phone turned off. On the verge of tears and feeling frightened and very alone, Karis decided to ring Bill and she was very relieved when he picked the phone up quickly. "Hello Bill. It's Karis. I'm sorry to bother you but I was doing some gardening and I've managed to hurt my shoulder and I don't know what to do. It's really painful."

"I'll come round. Be with you in ten minutes. Don't go away!" Karis smiled to herself. Thank God. Was she making a mountain out of a molehill? It was probably only a wrench and it would be OK as soon as he arrived. She was having second thoughts about ringing him. He would no doubt think she was a big baby.

Ten minutes later she heard the car draw up outside the house and she walked to the door to let him in, breathing out a big sigh of relief as she did so. "Bill. I'm sorry to be such a big girl's blouse but it really, really hurts and I've been almost dizzy with the pain. Thank you for coming. I rang Jonathan but he wasn't in and I didn't know who else to ask for help. I don't think it's broken otherwise I would have called the emergency services..." her voice broke and she sniffed as tears filled her eyes "I'm gabbling. Sorry."

"OK! Now, no more sorrys." He smiled at her, and his voice was gentle and reassuring as he took her left arm and walked her slowly into the kitchen and sat her down. "Now, let the nice doctor take a proper look at you and see what you've done to yourself." His voice, cool and calm, had a soothing effect on her. Gently he felt the shoulder with his fingers and then rotated her arm in the socket. "I may be a mind doctor but I think I can reassure you that you've not broken or dislocated the shoulder but it is possible, I think, that you may have pulled a ligament which, I know, is very painful and you will not be able to use your arm properly for a few days. There's nothing you can do about it but take some pain killers and rest it as much as possible. It will, though, take time to heal and if it doesn't improve in a couple of weeks, it may need a cortisone shot to help with the healing process and that means a visit to your doctor. Now, where can I find the pain killers?"

"Thanks, Bill. It's very comforting to know that it isn't dislocated although it felt like it when it happened. I'm grateful to you for coming to my rescue; I don't know what I would have done without you except weep like a child."

Just then there was the sound of a car pulling up outside the house and then quick footsteps to the front door and Jon's voice asking her to let him in. Karis looked at Bill who was looking slightly apprehensive.

"Could you let him in please, Bill? He must have got my text."

Jonathan's face registered surprise when the door was opened not by Karis as he expected but by a man he had never seen before. "I've come to see Karis, apparently she has hurt her shoulder. Who are you?" His voice was hostile.

"Bill Matthews. I am a doctor at the hospital where Karis works and she phoned me when she couldn't get any answer from either your landline or your mobile and she needed to see someone." His voice was calm and measured and not in the least hostile. He stepped to one side to let Jonathan into the house.

"Karis! What have you been doing to yourself? Is it bad? Do you need to go to hospital?" Jon bent and kissed her on the cheek, giving the impression that he was in charge and there was no need for anyone else to be there.

"No. The pain was so excruciating I thought I'd broken my shoulder, or at least dislocated it, but Bill says I've done neither, just pulled a ligament which sounds much less painful but, in fact, is causing me extreme discomfort. He was just about to get me some pain killers." Turning to Bill she said he'd find the tablets in the medicine cabinet in the bathroom.

Jonathan looked at Bill. "You're a doctor then? A GP?" And without waiting for his reply said he would get the pain killers for Karis and rushed upstairs to the bathroom.

Bill smiled at Karis. "I think he may have a bit of a guilty conscience not picking up your message sooner. Do you want me to stay or shall I go?"

"Please stay. I feel so much better now you're here and I don't expect Jonathan will stay for long. Would you like a drink or some tea?"

"I'll make a fresh pot of tea. I know where everything is and there is nothing like tea to sooth the nerves and quench the thirst."

By this time, having company, Karis was feeling slightly better, less frightened and more relaxed but also a little shame-faced at her initial reaction to her shoulder problem. And then she smiled to herself when she thought that she had waited a couple of hours for a man to come along and help and then two came along together!

Jonathan handed her the pain killers, with a glass of water, which she swallowed quickly. "I'm feeling better already and Bill is making some tea. Would you like a cup? I'm sure I'll be fine as soon as the pills take effect."

There was a slightly uneasy atmosphere while the three of them drank their tea and Jonathan was looking at Bill as if he had no right to be there. "I expect, being a doctor, you are busy so if you've got things to do, I'll stay and look after Karis and make sure she is OK. Are you sure she doesn't need to go to A&E?" His voice was still hostile.

"Quite sure. With an injury like this, there is nothing that can be done but to rest and take pain killers so a trip to A&E would just add unnecessary stress. Karis, my advice is to stay home for a few days but ring me tomorrow and let me know how you are. We can muddle through without you for a little while but, hopefully, the shoulder will respond to rest and then some physio, when you are ready for it, should see you as right as rain again within a week or so. So, now you've got some company to look after you, I'll be on my way." He smiled at Karis, nodded to Jonathan and left.

"Sorry I wasn't in when you rang, Karis. I was out on the golf course so, of course, I had my mobile switched off and didn't pick up your text until we got to the 19th. Now, I don't expect you've had much to eat, can I get you something? Louise has asked me round for supper this evening so I shall have to leave late afternoon so I've got time for a shower and a change of clothes but I've got plenty of time until then. What'll it be, beans on toast or Welsh rarebit or have you got a ready meal I can pop in the microwave?" So much for keeping me company Karis thought; I bet Bill would have stayed with me if I'd asked him and without him making the excuse that he had to go as he had other things to see to.

"Just some toast and cheese please Jonathan. I'm sorry to be a nuisance but I am feeling rather hungry now I've got over the shock so if you'd like to get me a snack then please feel free to leave whenever you want to. I shan't do anything else today except sit and nurse my shoulder and read the paper or watch TV and I can do that very well on my own thanks. I don't want to upset any arrangements you've already made." Perish the thought! When, she wondered, was the last time he'd put himself out for her?

"OK then. Toast and cheese it is." He appeared relieved that he wasn't expected to stay with her and whistled cheerfully, if somewhat out of tune, while he prepared her snack.

Karis tried watching TV that evening but found she couldn't concentrate on the whodunit that was being shown so switched off and tried reading the paper instead. But that was difficult to manage so she gave up on that too and just sat and listened to music on Classic FM, letting her thoughts drift over the day's events.

How can she have been so stupid to have damaged her shoulder so badly and why hadn't she waited for help to move the wretched hydrangea? Help from whom though? The postman? It was just one of those annoying things that occur when living on your own and not always being able to do the things that you wanted to because you needed another pair of hands. She should have left the bloody plant where it was instead of trying to be so stupidly self-sufficient.

And wasn't it just typical of Bill – immediate response to a call for help; and where would she be if he hadn't come round in answer to her plea? Whisked off to A&E the minute Jonathan had arrived so that he could pass the emergency on to someone else. That's not quite fair, she argued with herself, after all he had come as soon as he got her message, yes, and left as soon as he could to go and have supper with his girlfriend!

Well, that told her something didn't it? She was definitely no longer number one in his life. But how much did that hurt? There was no denying that since Jonathan had left he had given every appearance of being content with his lot and even though he was probably still fond of her, she felt it was unlikely that they would ever again experience the deep feelings they had had for each other for such a long time.

So how do I feel about that? Karis asked herself. No longer did she feel the ache of loneliness or the feeling of rejection that she had experienced every night when going to bed when Jonathan had first left and she had had the time to indulge in self-pity. Mostly now, her life was fairly full, principally with work but also with looking after the house, and definitely seeing Bill out of work hours had given her a new purpose and meaning and a reason for living and having fun. She realised that she had grown very fond of him and smiled to herself when recalling how quickly he had come to her aid this afternoon, pleased she thought to ring him and anxious to make her feel better. But was he just being professional, a good friend, or was he as fond of her as she was of him? Questions. Questions. How could she find out the answers?

Getting undressed and out of her clothes proved a bigger challenge than Karis expected but she managed it by various manipulations and manoeuvres, sliding into bed and sighing with relief once she was under the duvet. She had always been ambidextrous, using her left arm as much as she could when doing ordinary chores and also writing with her left hand just in case one day she couldn't use her right so this proved to be a great help now her right arm was almost useless. The shoulder had settled down to a dull ache but after the initial excruciating pain Karis felt she would be able to cope and swallowing two more tablets, she closed her eyes and fell asleep within a very short time and, for a change, her sleep was unbroken and dreamless.

Chapter 26

Within a couple of days, Karis found that her shoulder was feeling much better. Jamie and Joanne rang, commiserated with her on her accident and both of them telling her off for trying to do too much on her own. Joanne said that she would be over at the weekend to check her out and decide what physio she needed to do to help her shoulder repair and get better. Apparently, Jonathan had telephoned them with the news which rather surprised Karis and pleased her at the same time; perhaps he did care after all. Or maybe he was hoping that if either of them visited her at the weekend, there would be no need for him to call as well. I must stop having these nasty thoughts and being so cynical she thought.

In fact, Jonathan rang on Monday evening to enquire how she was although there was no offer to call round to see her, and Bill also telephoned on Monday evening to find out how she was getting on and also to ask if she needed anything, if she had enough food etc. and to tell her that all was well at work and that she wasn't to even think of hurrying back.

Bill called round on Tuesday evening with a bag of groceries, a paperback and a bottle of wine saying that he thought that by now she was probably going through withdrawal symptoms so he thought he should help out with some alcoholic medicine.

Karis was touched by his thoughtfulness and more than pleased to see him, her face lighting up when she saw him standing on the doorstep, and then feeling very pleased when he also gave her a bunch of pink roses. "Thought you might like these," he said.

"Thank you, Bill. They're lovely. And a bottle of wine! You really know how to spoil a girl." Karis felt overwhelmed. "And you couldn't be more right about my withdrawal symptoms so I am more than ready for a nice glass of wine. I've been very good and not had any wine at all, preferring to get the full benefit from the painkillers but I must admit I'm really going to enjoy this." She handed him two wine glasses and watched as he poured, impatiently waiting to try it.

"How's the shoulder? Feeling slightly better now?" Bill handed her a glass and took a sip of wine before looking enquiringly into her eyes as if he could read the answer there.

"Mmm. Much better, thanks. I can't raise my arm above elbow height yet but as long as I am careful and don't bang into anything and jar my arm then it doesn't feel too bad at all. In fact, in truth, I am feeling a bit of a fraud. I shall definitely be back at work next week. Joanne is coming over on Saturday to go through some physio with me which should also help to get me going again, so, I am feeling much more positive. And seeing you, too, is a bonus." Should she tell him how much she appreciated his calling round? In fact, she couldn't believe how pleased she felt.

They sat and chatted for a while and then Bill said that he had picked up a chicken in white wine ready meal so, if she hadn't eaten, perhaps they could share it and, if that suited madam, he'd put it in the microwave.

"Bill, that is so thoughtful of you. I've been very lazy and haven't eaten much except cereals and bananas and cheese and biscuits, all the wrong things in fact, so a hot meal will go down beautifully. You are a sweetheart to think of it."

Bill grimaced. "Just a man who likes to eat, I'm afraid. I'll go along with the saying that the way to a man's heart is through his stomach." He had his back to her while he was putting the meal into the oven so Karis couldn't see his face. Was he telling her something or was she reading too much into it?

They chatted easily while eating the chicken, which was surprisingly good, Bill obviously familiar with using a microwave and finding the necessary cutlery, plates etc. by opening drawers and cupboards, all the time passing on bits of gossip from the girls in the office and also their best wishes and to tell her not to hurry back as they were having a nice relaxing time without her setting such a high standard by working so hard all the time which meant that they had to work hard too to keep up!

"There you are then. What am I always telling you? You must learn to slow down a bit and not try to do everything at a hundred miles an hour. There's always tomorrow!"

"But is there? Tomorrow, that is?" Karis grinned at him. "OK Bill, I hear what you say. Please tell Jill and Angela to make the most of it while I am away and also thank them for the card. It was kind of them to think of me since I am such a hard task-master."

Bill collected their plates and put them in the dishwasher and then, raised the bottle of wine and looked enquiringly at her, "Silly question," he said to himself as he poured her another glass.

"I'm going to see my sister tomorrow evening but, if you like, I can come round again on Thursday evening, bring another ready meal or, how about fish and chips? Do you like them? There's so much about you that I don't know!"

"Yes I do like them and fish and chips would be lovely, thanks Bill. That's a great idea. What else would you like to know?"

"I'll make a list and ask you on Thursday. First I have to find a piece of paper long enough." He smiled at her, his eyes telling her that he cared about her. "Now, I'd better get going and let my patient have a good night's sleep. I'm glad you are doing so well. Ring me if you think of anything else you want me to bring on Thursday; I should be with you around 7.30ish. Take care of yourself until then. Don't get up - I can let myself out." And he bent down and kissed her on both cheeks.

Karis felt her breath catch in her throat. At last! A tangible sign of affection. Not exactly what she wanted but it was a step in the right direction. She smiled back at him.

"Thanks so much, Bill, for looking after me. I can't tell you how good it feels to be spoiled and to have someone make a fuss of me again and I really appreciate it. I'll ring you if I need anything. Please give my best to your sister and I shall look forward, very much, to seeing you on Thursday." She put out her hand and squeezed his arm and he briefly covered her hand with his. Somehow, it felt more erotic than if he had kissed her on the mouth.

Chapter 27

Karis heard Joanne coming before she saw the car pull up outside the house; obviously there was trouble with the exhaust. "Hi, darling! I think you need to visit the car doctor before you have a major problem," she said as she opened the door to let her daughter in. They embraced warmly.

"I know. Hello Mum. Are you feeling better now? The wretched exhaust started blowing a couple of days ago, just slightly but I'm afraid on the way here it got much worse and I think I'd better get it seen to before it blows up completely or I get reported for causing a disturbance with the noise." Joanne's knowledge of cars and what went on beneath the bonnet was about the same as her mother's - non-existent.

"The trouble is, I'm broke and it's going to cost a couple of hundred to put right, I expect, and I just don't have the money. And I'm trying to save up for the wedding and why is it that nothing is ever just right? Something always goes wrong to upset the applecart." She suddenly grinned at Karis, her face lighting up. "Sorry, Mum. Just me having a moan. Things aren't really that bad. It's not like I've had an accident or anything is it? How's the shoulder coming along?"

Karis felt like she'd been hit by a whirlwind which was typical of Joanne's arrivals; lots of noise and laughter, but she conceded to herself that she wouldn't have it any other way.

"The shoulder's much better, thank you darling. A few of your gentle exercises and I shall be right as rain. And perhaps I can help with the expenses of getting the car fixed. Kate gave me a cheque for helping her do some work recently and I haven't spent it so we can use some of that to get things mended for you. How about ringing the local garage now and seeing if they can do it this morning?"

"That's a good idea 'cos I'm not sure it would last long enough to see me home, apart from the embarrassment factor, that is. It is so noisy I can hardly hear myself think. It could also be dangerous, too, if the whole thing dropped off. But I will pay you back, of course, as soon as I can. What's the telephone number?"

Joanne busied herself telephoning the local garage, which had mechanics available Saturday mornings, and Karis could tell by her voice that she had a positive answer to her question. "They said that if I take it in now, they can fix it in a couple of hours. I'm just lucky that they have the right replacement in stock. So, I'll drive over now and walk back. Thanks, Mum. I'll take the car straight away and be back in a minute."

Karis was intrigued and a little puzzled by the exercises Joanne insisted would help her to recover her shoulder mobility but, since Joanne was the expert, she assumed that she knew what she was talking about. "I promise I'll do them faithfully, every day. When will it be fully mobile again do you think?"

"Probably another couple of weeks before it is completely better but you seem to be doing very well so far so, just leave the gardening alone and get Dad round here to help out when you've got something that needs doing that requires extra strength. How is he by the way?" Her tone was casual.

"He appears to be fit and well. He rang on Monday and again last night to see how I was but he hasn't called round since Sunday when I did the damage. And, frankly, Joanne, I think he has better things to do with his spare time."

Joanne glanced at her mother, pushing a lock of hair that had escaped from her pony-tail back into the pale blue scrunch that was made from the same material as her tee-shirt. "What do you mean? I'm surprised he's not here today to look after you." Joanne had always been a bit of a daddy's girl and she didn't take kindly to any criticism of him.

Karis hesitated, unsure whether to tell Joanne that he had a girlfriend and then deciding that she would find out sometime anyway, so she might as well know now.

"Your dad has a girlfriend, Joanne. A girl called Louise who works in the same office as he does. He introduced me to her when I bumped into them unexpectedly the last time I was in town shopping." Karis paused, briefly, looking to see how Joanne was taking the news, and then continued as she was not registering surprise or disbelief. "She's very pretty, with long, dark brown hair and she is also very pleasant. I confess that seeing them together did rather take me by surprise but I guess it's a natural thing to have happened. Your dad is an attractive man and I'd fancy him myself if I was in her shoes. Anyway, I don't think they are actually living together yet, although they obviously spend a lot of time in each other's company and their manner towards each other was very affectionate."

Joanne's facial expression had changed and was now a mixture of disbelief and sorrow. "I don't know what to say, Mum. I'm sorry. I've been so wrapped up in my own life with Lee that I confess I haven't given much thought to either you or Dad recently, although I always expected - still do in fact - that you would get back together again and that his leaving was only a temporary aberration while he recovered his equilibrium. Selfishly,

I'm still hoping that things will be back to normal by the time Lee and I get married next year. I shall, of course, want Dad to give me away and I hope that is not going to be a problem for you?"

"No, of course not, Jo, I was going to ask you about that, plus a lot of other things, too. We have a lot to discuss and talk about, the first thing being have you set a date for the wedding yet, where exactly are you planning to get married and will Lee's parents be home by then? There is so much to think about and plan for. I think that you must bring Lee home with you next time you come, although I expect his leisure hours are not always compatible with yours. Will he be staying on at the same hospital?"

"For the time being anyway, but there is a chance that he may go to another hospital in another part of the country in a year or two and then we both have a decision to make but that's very much in the future. But before we talk about the wedding, I want to talk about you and Dad. How do you really feel about Dad seeing another woman? I can't understand what he thinks he is doing. Can't he see that he is behaving badly and that you are bound to be upset by what is going on? I'd personally like to give her a piece of my mind so he'd better not let me see her or goodness knows what would happen." Joanne, who was soft-centred, was close to tears.

"Don't upset yourself, darling. I'm afraid that's just the way life is. It is seldom as we would like it to be and never, ever perfect. And, anyway, in the interim, I've become quite friendly with a doctor who works at the hospital where I work so I'm not in any position to pass judgement. He's a psychiatrist, very gentle and kind, and we've been out a few times together. He's been here twice this week, bringing me ready meals and fish and chips and I've enjoyed being spoiled and looked after. So, really, I can't say too much about Dad being friends with someone else because I'm pretty much in the same position myself."

Joanne was looking at her mother in disbelief. "I must say this morning is turning out to be a complete revelation! What else have you got to tell me? Is this the chap you told me you had a date with?" her voice rose slightly. "I suppose I ought to say good for you but what with Dad having an affair and you on the verge of also having an affair, I'm almost lost for words. You're our parents, for goodness sake! You're not expected to do things like that – well not my parents anyway. Does Jamie know?"

Karis listened to her daughter patiently, somewhat amused at her uncomplicated view of what life should be like. "Perhaps it's time to grow up a bit, Joanne," she said. "Your Dad and I are still young enough to want to enjoy our lives – if not with each other, then with someone else who makes us happy. I think it is possible that your father and I have reached the no going back stage in our relationship. It wasn't planned that way but it's happened. People change as they get older and we've grown apart, neither of us fulfilling the other one's idea of an ideal as we did when we were teenagers. And then you get an element of distrust creeping in and hey presto, the relationship as was has gone forever and will never be the same again. Cripes! Perhaps I should take up psychology."

Karis smiled fondly at her daughter. "Enough lecturing, I think. Just remember that few people are saints. And in answer to your question, Jamie sort of knows what the situation is I think. Now, how about we have some lunch and you can tell me all about your plans while we eat."

The worried frown that had been on Joanne's face faded away as she told her mother about her plans for her wedding, the words rushing out and tumbling over each other in her excitement, happiness now written all over her face. Karis listened, occasionally interjecting or asking a question but mostly just playing second fiddle to her daughter's lead; she was glad that Joanne was excited about her future and grateful to her for giving her something to think about and plan for. Remembering her own wedding brought nothing but the happiest of memories flooding back, she and Jonathan convinced that nothing, ever, would come between them and that they would sail into the sunset together still happily in love with each other.

Trying to apportion blame for their separation was useless, although, if asked, she would say that Jonathan's misuse of their money and his illness had something to do with it, whereas he would probably lay the blame squarely at the feet of Oliver for leaving her the money and a question mark, why?

Chapter 28

Karis went back to work the following Monday and then another week went by and the shoulder had almost completely healed, so much so that although careful when lifting things, Karis was thinking that it might be a good idea if she joined a tennis club, got a few games in and strengthened it further that way. She hadn't played for years but she was convinced that it was like riding a bike and that it would all come back once she had a racquet in her hand again. And, also, it might be a way of meeting some new people and making friends. The girls in the office were no help as neither of them was in the least bit interested in playing sport of any kind, disco dancing being their mode of exercise once a week so she asked Bill if he could recommend a club.

"You could try the Greenways Club," he said, "but the chances are they are fully or even over-subscribed at the moment and are likely to have a waiting list but it might be worth a try. My sister used to be a member but gave up when she had the family and she hasn't played for some time now. Tennis was never my game, as I was more interested in team sports. Why don't you give them a ring? And, how about coming out with me for dinner tomorrow evening? There's a bit of a cabaret at the Compass tomorrow night, with a local girl singing. Apparently, word has it that she is very good but, also, the food is usually pretty good too. Do you fancy that?"

"Thanks, Bill. I'd like that a lot. What time?"

The cabaret was much better than anticipated and, although amateur, sounded to both of them to be very professional, the girl having a lovely bluesy voice, seducing her audience with her singing. Bill said he wasn't a blues man but he gave every appearance of being enthralled and clapped enthusiastically.

The evening had gone well and there was a pleasant relaxed feeling between them, and Karis wondered if this would be the evening when their relationship moved up a gear. "Let's dance," she said as the cabaret act finished and the quartet resumed the easy listening and dancing to music that was typical of most clubs.

"OK. But you know I'm no good at dancing, mainly because I've got two left feet."

"Good enough to put your arms around me and hold on tight, I think, not to mention keeping me upright. I'm afraid the wine has gone to my head which seems to be entirely unconnected to my feet. Comes from not drinking for a while; I feel vaguely intoxicated and it's a lovely, relaxed feeling."

They swayed together on the floor, slightly moving their feet but dancing didn't come even close. Karis closed her eyes and enjoyed the sensation of being held closely in a man's arms again, breathing in Bill's aftershave and wanting the moment to go on and on. Did he feel the same way as she did? And what did she feel anyway? Was it love? Lust? Or was it just a feeling of being cherished? The music ended before she had made up her mind.

"I think, perhaps, it's time to go home, young lady. We've got work tomorrow and it's getting late but I'm glad you enjoyed the cabaret. We can come again if you'd like to, and always assuming they book her for another show."

Bill carefully saw Karis into the passenger's seat, putting the seatbelt on for her and making sure her long skirt was tucked in before shutting the door and driving to her house. "Please come in for a coffee Bill. I put it all ready before I left."

"Just a quick cup then, Karis, as I've a busy day ahead of me tomorrow."

"That'll make a change then, wont it? Tell me when you don't have a busy day. You work far too hard but I know you love your work so I don't expect you to be anything other than busy."

Karis busied herself with making the coffee and then serving it to Bill, who was watching her closely. "It was a lovely evening, Bill. Thank you. You are always treating me. How can I repay you?" She smiled at him.

"No need. I'm more than happy as things are. You'll have gathered that I am not particularly a lady's man, which is probably why my wife left me all those years ago," he made a face. "Not enough sex for her, I'm afraid, after the frenzy of our first few months together. To be honest, Karis, I'm not that interested and I'd better be honest with you, I have absolutely no intention of ever getting married again." He sighed. "I hope I haven't misled you but I thought we could just enjoy a nice platonic friendship, as I gathered you were still in love with your husband anyway. Was I wrong?"

Karis was dumbfounded by his words, her face registering her surprise but after hesitating for a moment, she decided that as he had been straight with her, she would say what she felt too.

"Yes. You are. Usually when a man asks a woman out it's because he likes her and I thought you liked me. I think you might have dropped me a hint before now. I feel very stupid for thinking that we might have been at the start of a relationship, although, thinking about it I realise now that you've never so much as made any attempt to kiss me properly let alone make love to me; I just thought that you were taking things slowly. I should have guessed you were not interested in me in that way. You are not gay are you?"

"No, I'm not. But neither am I bothered much about sex. I'm sorry I didn't tell you before now. I should have made things clear to you but we've always had lots to talk about and I've enjoyed your company very much so I thought we could just go on the way we were. Sorry, Karis. Does this mean that you want to finish our friendship?"

Karis looked at her feet, trying to sort out her feelings and not quite sure how to react to Bill's disclosure. Did it matter? What difference did it make anyway? Surely it was possible for two grown up people to have a platonic relationship because they liked each other without the question of sex coming into it? Was it a blow to her femininity, or her pride, that a man she was mentally willing to have a sexual relationship with her had made it clear that it just wasn't an option? Should she feel rejected? And the surprising thing was that, being honest, it wasn't a problem at all. In fact, it was something of a relief. She wouldn't have to go on wondering when or if, he was likely to make a pass at her, and she could just revert to being herself instead of acting like a lovesick teenager!

"No, of course not, Bill." Karis managed a smile. "There's no reason why we can't go to a show now and again, or even just for a drink and an argument - we're good at that at least!"

"That's a relief then." Bill smiled at her, putting out his hand and touching her arm. "I should be very sad if you said you didn't want anything more to do with me. My sister would be very happy to see me married again as she cannot understand my lifestyle at all and I know she thinks you would make me a wonderful wife. I've tried to tell her that it is not for me but, as you know, having met her, she always knows what is best for everyone and consequently doesn't take happily to her ideas not being accepted."

They sat looking at each other, both solemn and each lost in their own thoughts. "Well, that's that then. We'll just go along as we are now, both of us understanding the other and enjoying the moment, no commitment except as good friends, no worries either, just being there for each other when needed. We'll prove to everyone that it can be done – a platonic friendship that is as good as it gets." Karis felt that she had summed it up pretty well.

"Couldn't have put it better myself. Can't tell you how much better I feel for having got it off my chest, Karis. It's been worrying me for some time now and I'm really grateful to you for taking it the way you have."

Karis smiled at him, suddenly tired and wanting to go to bed, alone. "I like you so much, Bill. I'd rather have you as a friend than not have anything to do with you at all. It is time for you to go, I think. Thank you for a lovely, if somewhat surprising, evening."

"Trust you to say the right thing and I want you to know that I value our friendship more than you know. Goodnight, Karis. See you tomorrow."

Karis poured herself a single malt whisky and then sat on the sofa and relaxed. Her mind was too full of questions that had no answers and thoughts of what might have been, what might still be and where she was going with her life for her to be able to sleep. With a bit of luck the whisky would dull the thought process and she would be able to sleep when she went to bed in a while but in the meantime, she needed to just let her brain roam free.

Why hadn't Bill dropped a hint before now? Perhaps he had but it had been too subtle and she had been too dense to pick up on it. She should have realised that he wasn't exactly acting in the usual male manner when she had practically thrown herself at him a couple of times and he hadn't taken the bait. And yet, it had felt so right when he had held her in his arms when they danced and she was ready and willing to take him to bed. She should have known better but love, as everyone knows, makes fools of us all.

Love? No. Lust? No again. What then? Confirmation that she was a desirable woman in need of a man? Maybe, but she wasn't sure about that either as the more she thought about it the more she became convinced that it was probably just a vanity thing and she needed the reassurance of being wanted, or needed, having been rejected by her husband. She smiled to herself. Oh well, I'll just have to get over it and enjoy the freedom of being on my own; heaven knows there were plenty of pluses in that situation.

The whisky was both soothing and warming. Perhaps she would sleep now. To all intents and purposes, her life when she woke in the morning would not have changed at all, everything going along as it usually did, uneventful, predictable and also, she admitted ruefully to herself, just slightly dull.

Chapter 29

Tomorrow

Karis dressed carefully in the morning, determined to show Bill, and the world, that all was well with Karis Fielden. If she had worried that things between her and Bill would be awkward when they first saw each other after their conversation last night then that worry was unwarranted. He gave her a cheery smile and a hello when they met in the corridor at the hospital, as if everything between them was exactly as it had been and she answered him in the same vein to reassure him that it was. Not a problem at all.

She breathed a sigh of relief and was particularly chatty and cheerful with everyone else that morning which, as she was usually fairly quiet, raised a few eyebrows. Karis was aware of this and made a conscious effort to try and act as she usually did.

The day passed uneventfully as did the following weeks and months, life continuing in a fairly quiet and peaceful way. Karis joined a tennis club and was soon getting back into being a half-decent player. Her shoulder gave her no trouble at all and the extra exercise contributed to her losing a little bit of weight and feeling very fit and well. She and Bill met occasionally for a drink at the pub, each of them enjoying the other's company, particularly so now that they both knew exactly where they stood regarding their friendship.

Joanne's plans for the wedding were going ahead and she and Lee either telephoned her weekly or called round on a monthly basis to update her with what they were doing or what they had booked so far, reassuring her that they had the finances well under control. This bothered Karis. She had very little money to spare after she paid the bills on the house as she was still working only three days a week but she was anxious that she should make a contribution to the cost of the wedding and was wondering how she could do it, even though she knew that it was just a matter of pride and she had no need to worry as Joanne and Lee had their expected expenditure under control.

Karis had talked things over with Jonathan when they had had a family get together and as he was still living in rented accommodation and had his half share of the proceeds from the house he was in a position to make a reasonable contribution and she was anxious to match it, if possible.

Of course she had the money Kate had given her in the bank, which she had only touched to pay for Joanne's exhaust repair so she had that to fall back on; between them all they would be able to pay for the reception.

Karis was pleased, and relieved, that Joanne and Lee had chosen to have a fairly small wedding, only fifty guests, but the venue for the wedding breakfast was a lovely country hotel and would not be cheap. And then Lee had told them that his parents, who were due back from their world trip a month or so before the wedding, were insisting that they pay half of the costs of the wedding, which was a further bonus and a great relief to Karis who, on hearing the good news, decided she would give up worrying about it.

Karis's meetings with Jonathan were few and far between, although they had probably met more than they would have done if Joanne's wedding hadn't given them a reason to meet, discuss and decide various things about it. And then, one day out of the blue, Jonathan rang and said he wanted to see her as he had something he wanted to discuss, could he come round on Sunday morning and since Karis had, as usual, nothing planned, she invited him for lunch which to her surprise he accepted without hesitation.

The chicken curry was reheating nicely in the oven and giving off a very pleasant spicy aroma when Jonathan arrived, smiling and sniffing the air in appreciation.

"Chicken curry for Sunday lunch! How lovely. You made it yourself, of course," he added, kissing her briefly on each cheek. "How are you? You're looking good. Have you lost some weight?"

"Yes. Fine. Thank you and yes in answer to all your questions. I don't usually bother to make curry for myself so cooking for someone to share with me gave me the excuse I needed. And I'm looking forward to it too. Would you like a coffee or a beer?" It almost felt like old times.

"Oh, beer, please. It'll go nicely with the curry. Can I help with opening it? And are you having one too?"

"Yes, please." Karis opened the fridge and took out two bottles of beer and put them on the table. "As it is such a nice warm day, I thought we could sit in the garden while the rice is cooking. OK? In fact, I think we'll eat al fresco too. What do you think?"

"Yes. Good idea. I must admit that I miss having a garden. It's not as if I can't go into our shared space if I want to, but the fact that it is shared puts me off. And it is a long way from being as secluded and peaceful as this. It's looking very good, Karis. Is there anything I can help with while I am here?"

He looked around the small paved square, noticing the wooden tubs full of salmon pink geraniums and the climbing honeysuckles and clematis that were in full bloom. "It all looks lovely, and very quiet and peaceful." He sipped his beer and looked at Karis over the rim of the glass, his blue eyes smiling at her. "Cheers, Karis. This is just like old times."

Karis smiled back and thought to herself, no it isn't! We used to be in love, we used to be married and although we are still married, love has flown out of the window so it isn't like old times at all. What did he want to talk to her about? Was he going to ask her for a divorce? While she pondered the question, she changed the subject completely and asked him if he had been watching the cricket.

"No. Unfortunately, I haven't got Sky so I haven't seen any of the test matches. I suppose you've been glued to the box?"

The talk between them was of little or no consequence and Karis felt that the atmosphere was slightly strained and even though Jonathan appeared relaxed, she felt that he was not completely at ease. Oh well, just wait and I guess I'll find out soon enough what it's all about, she thought.

Their conversation continued while they ate the chicken curry and all the bits and pieces that Karis had prepared to go with it, mango and banana, spring onions and tomatoes, nuts and desiccated coconut. "This is really very good, Karis. Any chance of seconds?"

Jonathan was obviously enjoying the food; whether it was because he hadn't had to get it for himself or just because he liked curry, Karis hadn't a clue, although she was pleased he had voiced his appreciation which made her feel her efforts had been worthwhile. "Yes, of course. Please help yourself."

After Jonathan had finished his second helping of curry and then polished off two slices of lemon tart, Karis made the coffee and they moved into the sitting room. Deciding there had been enough pussy-footing around, Karis took a sip of her coffee and then asked Jonathan what it was he wanted to discuss with her, looking expectantly at him as she did so.

For a moment or two, he looked surprised but then he smiled weakly at her and said, "I've been doing a great deal of thinking lately, Karis, the result, of spending so much time by myself, I guess, and I've gradually come to realise that I've been a complete fool, a stupid, idiotic fool. Why I left you in the first place I don't know. It's not as though you deserved to be treated so badly by me. It's just that I was madly jealous, out of control jealous and I wanted to hurt you as I thought you had hurt me. Karis, it hasn't worked out between Louise and me and, if I am honest, I never thought it would. I was living in a fool's paradise, trying to convince myself that I still had what it took to make a younger woman fall in love with me, trying to get back at you. I was so wrong. Could you, would you, consider giving me another chance? Will you, please, let me back into your life and let me try to make up to you for all the hurt I've caused you?"

Karis stared at him, completely taken by surprise. So that was what it was all about! Whatever it was that Karis thought he was going to ask her it certainly wasn't that. The last time she had seen him he had appeared to be happy and content with his new life and his getting back to living with her again had never occurred to her. The surprise showed on her face.

"Do you think you've given it a fair crack of the whip, Jon? You've hardly been with Louise for more than a year or so." Why did she feel as if she was talking to one of her children? "If it was me, I'd feel very fed up with being given the bum's rush after such a short time. How does Louise feel?"

"Well, it was sort of mutual between us, both of us agreeing that we had given it our best shot and deciding that we had no real future together. I guess the main stumbling block to us continuing was that she wanted to have children and, frankly, I feel I am too old to want to start another family..." his voice trailed off. "And I miss you, Karis. I miss you so much."

Karis laughed. "You miss me. Well that's nice! Did you ever think that maybe I would miss you when you upped sticks and left me without a backward glance? I suppose I should feel flattered. What bit of me did you miss most, I wonder? The cooking? The nicely ironed shirts? My ability to balance the books when the funds were low or non-existent? My support for you when you were ill and in desperate need of TLC? Honestly, words fail me! And now you'd like to come back, please, for all the world as if you've just been out getting the paper from the local shop!"

Jonathan was looking horrified. "You may well look surprised, Jon. I've changed a bit since we were living together; I've learned to be truly independent and, in case you're interested, it hasn't been at all easy. There have been lots of times when I've felt like giving up and giving in to my feelings of despair, feeling unloved, discarded and unwanted. How do you think I felt when you walked out on me, in fact, did you think at all about the effect it would have on me? No? Thought not. Well, for the record, I've got used to being on my own and I like it and I'm not at all sure that I shall ever want to live with anyone ever again."

"What about Bill? Surely you're good friends with him. I thought that perhaps you liked him enough to want to be in a relationship with him, or maybe live

241

together." Jonathan was determined not to feel too much of a heel and to somehow justify his reason for leaving.

"Bill and I are in a relationship. It's called friendship. Pure and simple. We have a drink together and sometimes we have a game of tennis. I know what you're thinking, there is no such thing as a platonic relationship between a man and a woman but in this particular instance, you are wrong. There is."

Jonathan was looking sceptical but he wasn't going to give up. "So there is no chance for me to come home then, even though Joanne will be getting married from here next year and I shall be giving her away?"

"That's typical of you, Jonathan, playing on our family ties. But I don't think you have given that much thought until now, have you? And it makes no difference to our situation as far as I can see. Joanne's wedding will happen the way she wants it to even if we are not living together."

"But you've never mentioned getting a separation or a divorce. Is that what you want?" Jonathan was beginning to feel he was losing the argument when, truthfully, he hadn't expected any opposition to his suggestion that he should return home.

"No. I haven't and that is mainly because I've never thought that far ahead. But things and circumstances change; nothing stays the same forever so maybe it is something we should seriously consider."

The optimism in Jonathan's voice had faded. He couldn't believe that Karis was not going to have him instantly back in her home and back in her life. He had obviously misunderstood or misread her nature, and he thought he knew her so well. Perhaps he should give her more time to think things through when, surely, she would come to appreciate the benefits his return would bring.

As if reading his mind, Karis said, "At the moment, I can see no possible reason why I should have you back. In fact, the constraints outweigh the benefits and how am I to know that it won't happen again when you see another pretty face who you think needs a helping hand to help her cope, not to mention, warm her bed."

"That's not fair, Karis! We've spent the best part of our lives together and I've never even looked at another woman until Louise came into my life and I genuinely liked her, it wasn't just some passing fancy. But she has been the only one. And what about you? You haven't been a saint have you, by your own admission."

"No. I haven't. Saints live in heaven – there aren't many on earth. But neither did I deserve the treatment you dished out to me either, and never, even when in the depths of despair when life was at a very low ebb, did I ever consider leaving you. So now we've gone full circle and I can't see any good reason to go on with this conversation. Perhaps a cup of tea would help to calm our frayed nerves. Would you like one?"

"It would help if you weren't so damned practical and sensible but, yes, a cup of tea would be good." He had nowhere to go anyway except an empty, cheerless flat; the thought immediately produced another drop in his spirits. He decided to have one last appeal to his wife. "Please think about it, Karis. You know I've always loved you, and in spite of what has happened over the last few years, I always will. I think you owe me a second chance."

Karis lay in her bed, snuggled up under the duvet, with a book open waiting for her to start to read. She was comfortable and warm, cosy even and looking forward to her evening read. It was a good story and she was not feeling tired, although she felt uneasy and troubled by what Jonathan had said to her and also more than a little upset by her response to him, which had taken her by surprise as much as it had him. She thought she would probably read well into the night to take her mind off things.

Jonathan's appeal to her to have him back had taken her completely by surprise; in a way it would have been better if she had had pre-warning of what he was going to say when, in fact, it was the reverse of what she had been expecting.

Maybe, then, if she'd had a chance to think things through her answer would have been different but she didn't think so. It was not that she didn't love Jonathan, she did, but the love she had felt for him early on when they were kids was now something completely different and there was no doubt that his affair had shaken her because it had appeared to be so deliberate as if part of his plan to punish her. There was no doubt that she missed his physical love, his caress and the way he would touch her hair when passing close by, smiling at her tenderly with love in his eyes. And she missed loving him too, caring for him and feeling the warmth of his body by her side at night.

She sighed deeply and picked up her book. I will give it some serious thought, but not tonight. Tomorrow.

Chapter 30

Yesterday

Suddenly, Karis was in Oliver's arms. His mouth was on hers and he was kissing her with such urgency and passion that she responded in spite of fleeting feelings of restraint. He half-pulled, half-dragged her into his office and locked the door behind her, his arms still wrapped around her. All the office staff had now left but the cleaning company would be in shortly and this, this, was private.

He kept his arms around her and they were both laughing as they fell in a heap onto the leather sofa; this was lunacy, this was madness even and it was such a surprise to them both that it felt as if it was happening to someone else. It surely couldn't be real.

Oliver caressed her body, his voice in her ear telling her how much he had always wanted to make love to her. It was if all the pent-up frustrations and emotions of the past few months had suddenly been unleashed. And yet he was gentle with her and she kissed him back, feeling that this was meant to be and that there was no turning back.

He was a considerate lover, tender but passionate. Karis gave herself up to the moment, knowing all the while that she would have regrets but being totally unable to stop the feeling of supreme pleasure that filled both her body and her mind.

Their return to normality and the sense of now happened quickly; both of them being suddenly overwhelmed with guilt and dismay.

"Oh my God, Karis! What have I done?" Oliver was distraught. "I'm afraid I had a rush of blood to the head. After all the hard work of the last few months it just seemed like a happy conclusion. I'm so sorry. I don't know what else to say to you." His face was a picture of abject dismay.

"Well, whatever you want to call it, you didn't do it on your own, Oliver. We are equally to blame." Karis adjusted her clothes and stood up, smoothing her hair as she did so.

"Let's just say that we got carried away with euphoria –whoever she might be!" She laughed. "I know I shouldn't joke but neither is it the end of the world either. As far as I am concerned, Oliver, this just didn't happen. We can put it in a box named secret and keep it there. No one else need ever know, we will get on with our lives as usual and we will never refer to it again. Agreed?"

"Practical and sensible and now I know you are sexy, too. Is there no end to your talent? You're right, though, Karis. It is our secret. No one else need ever know." He didn't say so but he wondered why she hadn't been angry and why she was letting him off so lightly. But he would keep it to himself that he would never ever regret their 'secret'.

Shortly afterwards they left the office together, and then went their separate ways, Karis to her daughter's school play and Oliver to his home and his beloved wife Kate, their lives inextricably changed forever.

*